11/22

"Peter Ter...

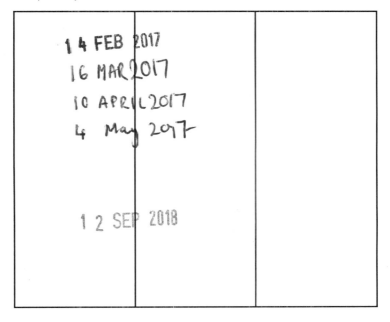

Shettleston Library
154 Wellshot Road
Glasgow G32 7AX
Phone: 0141 276 1643 Fax 276 1645

This book is due for return on or before the last date shown below. It may be renewed by telephone, personal application, fax or post, quoting this date, author, title and the book number

1 4 FEB 2017		
16 MAR 2017		
10 APRIL 2017		
4 May 2017		
1 2 SEP 2018		

Glasgow Life and its service brands, including Glasgow Libraries, (found at www.glasgowlife.org.uk) are operating names for Culture and Sport Glasgow

Glasgow
CITY COUNCIL

"... in a coldly beautiful, dystopian allegory depicts the world of now a serene place paralysed by an unspecified threat. ... This is a tremendous novel, often horrifically funny and always unsettling."
EILEEN BATTERSBY, *Irish Times*

"A strange, wonderfully claustrophobic novel ... A mix of S.F. fable and psychological thriller."
JOHN O'CONNELL, *Guardian*

"A dazzling work ... The Guard is so good, its world so undeniably compelling that to suggest anything other than to pick this up and read it immediately would be to do it a disservice."
DAN HOWELL, *S.F.Now*

"Concentrated and claustrophobic ... Two security guards with nothing to guard weave webs of Pinteresque paranoia. Almost comic at first, their obsession leads with fearful illogic to smoothly."
DAVID LANCYOVO, *Sunday Telegraph*

"The first of Peter Terrin's books translated for an English audience, and boy is it a good one... You won't want to put it down."
JOE KOKER, *Starburst*

"There's a cold and terrible precision to Peter Terrin's writing, and a remorseless and finally terrifying accretion of detail ... This parable is enough to send a shiver down your spine."
JON COURTENAY GRIMWOOD, *S.F.X.*

Peter Terrin

THE GUARD

Translated from the Dutch by
David Colmer

MACLEHOSE PRESS
QUERCUS · LONDON

First published in the Dutch language as *De Bewaker*
by De Arbeiderspers, Amsterdam, in 2009
First published in Great Britain in 2012 by MacLehose Press
This paperback edition published in 2013 by

MacLehose Press
an imprint of Quercus
55 Baker Street
7th Floor, South Block
London W1U 8EW

The translation of this book was funded by the
Flemish Literature Fund (www.flemishliterature.be)

A CIP catalogue record for this book is available
from the British Library.

ISBN (MMP) 978 1 84866 294 0
ISBN (Ebook) 978 0 85705 219 3

This book is a work of fiction. Names, characters,
businesses, organizations, places and events are either the
product of the author's imagination or are used fictitiously.
Any resemblance to actual persons, living or dead, events
or locales is entirely coincidental.

2 4 6 8 10 9 7 5 3 1

Designed and typeset in Goudy by Patty Rennie
Printed and bound in Great Britain by Clays Ltd, St Ives plc

FOR V. AND R.

ONE

1

"We have to see this through to the end."

Resupplying makes Harry nervous. Even though we know our way blindfold, he folds the basement floor plan out on the table: one hundred and twenty parking spaces spread over forty secure garages, one for each of the thousand-square-metre luxury apartments. It would have been smarter to make the basement a simple rectangle. Perhaps that wasn't possible because of the building's construction and foundations. I'm no engineer. Still, a rectangular design with the parking spaces arranged neatly down the long sides would have made security a lot simpler. Harry suspects that the irregular layout was designed to meet the clients' requirements. With comfort and privacy taking priority. You know how these things go, he says.

I catch a whiff of his agitation. The smell of walnut, fresh walnuts that have just fallen from the tree, with hard, green hulls. We study the floor plan together. I lay a hand on his shoulder, realize that's not a good idea and pull it back. It's quiet. Out of habit, I touch the weapon at my hip; there's no direct danger. I take a step to one side so that the bare bulb can light every corner of the plan.

"So he comes in here."

He points at the entrance, which is four metres wide and designed to withstand a missile impact. It's the building's only entrance. Apparently the ground floor is hermetically sealed: no windows or doors. For security reasons, we have neither a digital pass nor an infrared key, and the scanners don't recognize our fingerprints. We have to remain in the basement and guard the entrance at all times. Outside, on the other side of the gate, our authorization no longer applies.

"He'll open the gate and drive the van into the basement. You take up position at Garage 3. In clear view. Keeping him covered at all times. O.K.?"

I nod. "O.K."

"I'll ask for his I.D. and a confirmation. At my signal, you walk to the rear of the van. This is where it gets tricky. We have to be on our toes. When he swings open the doors, we have a fraction of a second to assess the situation."

"No time to talk," I add. "Each of us, separately, decides whether or not to open fire. But if one of us opens fire, the other joins in unconditionally."

Harry puts his hands in the small of his back and leans back with his head and shoulders to ease the tension in his spine. "Dead right," he says. When he bends forward again I see a loose thread in the seam of his uniform, a cheerful little curl poking out of the sharp line of his jacket, about twenty centimetres below his armpit. I don't mention it for now. I can do that later when we've gone through the plan in full detail. The rest of the plan comes first. Resupplying is just two days away.

2

I'm lying on the bunk bed, the bottom one, my pillowcase giving off the fresh smell of liquid soap. I will probably fall asleep soon. Our room is next to the first lift. There are only three lifts for forty floors: an extremely fast lift for the residents, an extremely fast service lift and a reasonably fast lift for visitors. Our room is small, but that is seldom, if ever, a problem. After all, we're always working. We sleep one after the other for five hours each. That's enough, we're trained for it. If one of us gets too tired, he can lie down for quarter of an hour. I can't recall it ever happening, but it's reassuring that the organization has taken the eventuality into account.

The door is half open, the glow of the emergency lighting, which starts five metres away, is visible on the bunkroom floor. Outside, far beyond this building's thick walls, it is quiet and peaceful. At least, I can't hear anything: no rumbling, no explosions, no uproar. Nothing at all. I can't feel any vibrations in the ground either. We don't have an overview of the situation from in here. It is impossible for us to imagine what the conditions outside are really like. They're actually irrelevant. Our task is here in the basement, at the entrance.

Harry is on watch, sitting on the chair next to the door. Now and then he stands up and walks around in a small circle. When he passes the doorway his shadow darkens the room. He checks the cartridge clip of his weapon, then slides it back into the magazine with a loud click. Although I can't see him, I know that he is extending his arm, holding the pistol out in front of him. Possibly supporting one hand with the other. His right eye trained on the bead and the sights, his index finger cradling the trigger.

3

I lay the steaming loaf on a tea towel on a plate to let it cool down. I use the bread maker almost every day; it's dead easy and the bread is delicious, well worth it. The machine is a cast-off from the Olano family apartment and was meant to go out with the rubbish.

I tell Harry he'll have to be patient.

Reluctantly, he walks out of the room to resume his position on the chair next to the door. A little later he pokes his head around the corner.

"You can smell it past Garage 4," he says.

Garage 4 is furthest away from our room.

"The smell of concrete's gone from the whole basement. It's like walking around in a giant loaf of bread."

I think about when I was little and dreamt about a bath that was filled to overflowing with chocolate milk. I didn't get out until I'd drunk it all. At school I kept sucking my fingers to get the faint, residual taste of chocolate from under my nails.

I notice that I'm hesitant about telling Harry about my dream, but can't immediately say why. Perhaps it's just because here, obviously, we have no access to chocolate.

4

The shiny toe of one of my shoes pops into the bottom of my field of vision every time I take a step. The blue trouser leg slides easily over the leather and fall backs into its crease. I count us very lucky that we found liquid soap and a good supply of shoe polish in the staff general storage area, an improvised cubicle on our floor. The products weren't intended for the residents' clothes and shoes, but for the personal use of the staff; that's why we thought it, given the circumstances, completely acceptable for us to use them too. Ordinary shoe polish and barrels of bleaching liquid soap without any particular perfume, unless it's the neutral smell of cleanliness.

Harry and I are walking alongside each other. We are following the perimeter of the open space in the middle of the basement, hardly cutting any corners, keeping our hands behind our backs. It's not strolling; the pace we maintain is slow but steady. We keep silent so that we can judge each noise correctly, quickly locating its source. Our caps, blue with the organization's emblem embroidered on the front, are perched on our heads at the prescribed angle. The length of our steps differs but now and then, involuntarily, we march in time for a couple of metres. The effect reminds me of pealing bells that disentangle more and more until all of the clappers strike the bronze together: just once, twice at most.

There was a time I counted my footsteps during every round

of inspection, over and over again. I counted them in my head and then added the result, in my head, to the previous total. I never wrote anything down. I think it was the dedication that appealed to me, the concentration. I thought it would hone my attention. I no longer count because the reverse was true: it distracted me from my work. All things considered, counting footsteps was an exercise in futility.

5

We complete three inspection rounds then take a break. Harry sits on the chair, I sit on the stool. We sit either side of the bunkroom door, which is ajar. Harry hasn't slept well; I heard him tossing and turning. The slight bags under his eyes won't go away. Last night I cut off the loose thread in the seam of his jacket. His uniform is back in tip-top condition, the way it should be.

"Shall we run through the resupplying again?" he asks.

"Seems like a good idea to me," I say.

We stay sitting there in the silence of the basement.

The emergency lighting is made up of sixteen light fittings on the ceiling and they all work, as dim as the tubes may be, which is nothing short of a miracle. With the exception of Number 22, all of the garages are closed. Remote controls are reserved for the apartment owners' personal assistants. It wasn't the first time Mrs Privalova's assistant forgot to close the garage after fetching the Bentley.

"The organization sometimes tests its own guards," Harry says.

"What do you mean?"

"You can count on it," he says. "It couldn't be any other way, if you think about it. Random checks, you know the kind of thing." He rubs his forehead with his right hand, thumb and fingers pushing the skin back and forth. "All businesses practise quality control. It's normal. Every business sets its own standards that have to be reached or maintained under all circumstances. Quality control is achieved through random checks. What is the organization, if not a business with a product?"

During my entire period of training I didn't hear a word about random checks. No-one ever mentioned it. That's why, after a few seconds, their existence seems very plausible.

Harry slides his cap back, then forwards again. "If the organization wants to secretly carry out random checks, I can only think of one possibility: standard situations."

He means resupplying, the only standard situation we deal with. He says, "We have to be twice as alert. In a way we have two enemies to fear."

I go into our room to get a piece of bread. Although I know that no-one can see me, I am very aware of my movements. Back on the stool, I chew the bread slowly. I look out over a bare concrete surface, extending approximately one hundred metres. I avoid looking into the darkness beyond it.

"The nice bit," Harry says suddenly, "what's clever of the organization, is that it's impossible for the random checks to ever come out. Either it ends well and everything's O.K. and no situation results, or it ends badly and, in that case, the incompetent guards were simply ambushed. You follow? Who in their right mind would accuse the organization of attacking its own men? Especially if there's casualties. Nobody, right!"

He smiles at his own conclusion.

At the same time his smile says it's an organization we can be proud to be a part of.

I ask about the elite, if they get tested too.

"You bet, Michel. I suspect they have even more random checks to deal with than we do . . . Of course they do, that goes without saying. The elite are the organization's calling card. The apex in security. That calling card has to be irreproachable. It can't have the slightest blemish. It has to be dazzling white."

He stands up and walks into the bunkroom, where he unfolds the basement floor plan. He's stopped smiling. "I can assure you that we will not miss out on promotion because of laxness during a standard situation." His voice sounds cold, as if I've insulted him. "That would be really stupid, don't you think, after all this time?"

6

I stick the key in the lock and turn it twice. The storeroom adjoins the bunkroom; this is my second inspection today. On the left, on three shelves attached to the wall with metal brackets, the boxes are arranged in battle order. Placed at right angles to the shelves, they are all marked Winchester. The calibre is printed on the short side: 9mm Luger (Parabellum). Above that, a cowboy gallops to the edge of the white box, his upper body leaving an orange trail, his horse, a red one. The brand name is printed in the red stripe, the letters sloping to the right as if caught in the horse's slipstream.

I see at a single glance that all of the boxes are present. I recognize the total picture, the complete array of ammunition. To be on the safe side, I count them, per shelf, my index finger brushing over the boxes. Three times fifteen makes forty-five.

I pick up the first box. Its weight in my hand feels right, familiar. It opens easily. After all this time, the box is loose around the flap. Gleaming cartridges, upright and neatly aligned, showing me multiple reflections of my silhouette. My index finger counts one row of five, then ten rows. Ten fives are fifty. I close the box, put it on the shelf and slide the second box out of the row. The weight feels right. The flap slips out with virtually no resistance.

After the inspection, I check the supplies on the shelves on the other wall. Our rationing is going according to plan. We still have one bottle of water left for the next twelve hours; we haven't touched the purification tablets. Shoe polish, liquid soap, toilet paper. Two kilos of powdered milk. We've used up the yeast and flour, but there's half a loaf of bread in our room.

I turn off the light and lock the door.

I inform Harry of the results of the count. We remove our Flock 28s from our hip holsters and take turns to push in the magazine catch and let the cartridge clip slide out of the pistol, counting the bullets in silence. After I've nodded to Harry, he repeats the result of my inspection out loud and says, "Plus two times fifteen."

7

I do the first part of the night, sitting on the chair and keeping still. After a while I detect a noise that is only just audible over the hum of the lights. When I turn my head towards my left shoulder, it fades. The acoustics in the basement are strange. I don't find it necessary to wake up Harry. It's a blessing he's been able to fall asleep.

I decide to do a round to keep my head clear and set off in the reverse direction; my footsteps echo back from the basement's furthest corners. When I stop, it takes a moment for the last echoes to die out. Surrounded by bare walls and with sounds bouncing back at me from all sides, would I be able to distinguish the steps of other feet if they were hitting the ground at the same time as mine?

As uncertain as my answer may be, the question doesn't disturb me: having asked it means I'm still thinking. I have a strong suspicion that bad guards eventually stop thinking about their situation. Habituation is a stealthy foe.

I put one eye to the narrow crack to the right of the entrance gate and peer through it. The missing sliver of concrete probably broke off while the steel groove for the gate was being mounted. As it's dark outside, I can hardly see a thing. What I think I can see is a product of my imagination; the view is imprinted on my memory. A section of wall tapering up to street level. Above it, a round treetop silhouetted against a patch of sky. The treetop reminds us of the seasons.

I press my nose against the gap, sniffing the cool breeze. The weather conditions are neutral. Smells carry better when it's hot or raining. I turn around and lean back on the wall. Again I get the creeping feeling that what I see from here would be the very first image of the basement to confront an intruder. I try to imagine the situation. His brain will most likely soak up the visual information like a sponge, immediately comparing it to the floor plan he has studied in advance. Or just trying to work out the direction of his next step if he's seized the opportunity unprepared. He mustn't get much further. The instant following the intruder's first observation of the basement should see him flat on the ground. Preferably dead with a bullet to the head.

I continue my round slowly, feeling confident. It's foolish, but rather pleasant. I could just as easily be walking in a park with my hands in my pockets. Enjoying the trees and bushes, sitting down on a bench. Closing my eyes for a moment.

8

I can hear it clearly, not over the noise of the emergency lighting as I first thought, but seeping through under it. I am sure I know what it is, that the knowledge is buried somewhere inside of me, that I've heard it before. It's a question of training my ear to it, being confident and not thinking about it. I suppress the urge to turn my head towards it; I can hear it well enough, I don't want to lose it. All at once, as if from the effort of resisting that impulse, a membrane inside me bursts and, as if it could never have been anything else, the answer presents itself. I can hardly believe I didn't recognize the sound of a leaking cistern. To be precise: the whistling sound of the toilet which, because of the leak, continues to draw water from the pipe.

9

I put my hands together behind my head and stare at the bottom of Harry's bunk, at the grid of crinkled wire, gleaming in the pale glow. I am immediately wide awake, my mind fresh and open.

When I groan loudly and swing my legs out of bed, Harry looks around the corner. Lit from behind, his face is black and impossible to read. Of course, he's trying to see if I'm properly awake and ready to get up.

"I'll just have a wash," I say.

"Excellent."

He pushes the door to our room almost shut.

I walk over to the washbasin and turn on the light, washing myself thoroughly and quickly; hot water is a luxury we can scarcely remember. After wringing out my flannel and laying it over the edge of the basin, I feel Harry's. It's still quite damp. Although there are only slight fluctuations of temperature in the basement through the year, it is now clearly growing colder. After five hours, the flannel is usually as stiff as an old chamois.

I put on my uniform: dark-blue trousers, leather belt with leather hip holster, light-blue shirt, black tie with a simple knot, black lace-ups, jacket, cap with a stiff peak and an embroidered emblem. I look in the mirror. My beard doesn't need trimming yet. I pop a piece of bread into my mouth, more for its cleansing effect than to still my hunger.

Harry is holding his pistol, his hand resting on his lap. He looks up; his cheeks are tense from constantly gritting his teeth and he blinks several times in quick, irregular succession. "I've already heard the gate start up ten times. You know what it's like when you're sitting here alone waiting."

We both look over at the other side of the basement. The gate is on the right, tucked in behind Garage 1. The walnut smell is so pungent I take a step away from Harry. Although, according to my watch, we have at least three hours to go before we can expect the van, I already feel the tension, whereas Harry relaxes a little now that I'm here to keep him company. At any rate, he holsters his weapon and lets out a deep breath.

"You think that guy's awake yet?"

"I doubt it," I say. "Not if he works in the daytime. They'll probably wake him up about an hour from now."

"An hour."

"Something like that."

"But it could be earlier?"

"It could be, definitely, that's possible. But I don't think so, to be honest. Not from what I remember from the period before they brought me here, no. I don't think so."

"So that guy's still just snoozing away."

"Most likely."

Five minutes later I raise a finger up next to my ear. "Hear that?"

Harry jumps. "What?" He scans the basement.

"That noise. Just under the sound of the emergency lighting."

Harry looks like he's pondering something deeply, a riddle. He's sitting on the chair, I'm on the stool, the door of the bunkroom is between us. On the edge of hundreds of square metres of emptiness that will soon come to life. We keep our uniforms neatly brushed, every day, because regulations are sacred. Harry and I are in complete agreement on that. After all, it's the uniform that makes the guard. The uniform and the weapon.

10

I keep my legs slightly spread; they're drained and wobbly. I feel as if the opening of the gate will be enough to knock me over. The moment the gate comes up off the ground, I'm blinded: as if it's been piling up against it since the last resupply, the sunlight floods in all at once. I take the blow front on. It knocks the breath out of me. I feel like turning away, my closed eyelids glow. I bow my head. I stretch the arm holding the pistol out in front of me. It might not look impressive, but it helps to keep me on my feet.

The van is driving into the basement. I know because the diesel engine is thundering between the walls and cramming the empty space with its presence. I resist this new assault on my senses. I can still hear the gate, but only vaguely; the movement has already reversed, it's getting dark again. The engine turns off with a clunk, having approached close to my knees. I blink, patches appear on my retina. The gate touches the concrete, the heavy segments press down on each other. Then it goes quiet. Quieter: under the bonnet the contracting metal clicks. I can also clearly hear the driver whistling and Harry panting as if he's been screaming at the top of his voice.

I recognize the van: it's the model the organization always uses. It does me good to see the familiar emblem in self-confident dimensions. We're members of a large, widespread family that boasts years of experience and has managed to survive through restless times. The bodywork looks newly cleaned and shows, as far as I can tell from a first glance, no signs of serious damage from the conditions outside. No traces of violence or anything like chemical fallout. Gleaming like an alien vehicle that has just landed unsuspectingly on earth, the van sits in the basement.

"What have we here?" the driver says after swinging the door open. "The welcoming committee. Everything O.K., guys?"

"Can it," Harry says from his position at the back of the van. "You know damn well what's expected of you. Keep your gob shut and unload."

The youth resumes his cheerful whistling while Harry's still talking and gets out of the cab, holding up the pass around his neck and the one in his other hand simultaneously. To my surprise he is once again out of uniform. I almost say something to Harry, but he's noticed it too, of course. Last time it was the middle of summer and it seemed plausible that he was in his shirtsleeves because of a new rule, unknown to us, that permitted drivers to remove their jackets during heatwaves. But now, although they are both the official shade of blue, I can't think of any logical explanation for his baggy top and unpressed trousers, and his trainers least of all. Is it even the same driver? They're all gawky and spotty, you can hardly tell them apart. They all start on resupply.

I don't like those trainers. What's more, they're squeaky clean, without a splash of mud, and that for a driver who has to go to the most unlikely places. My hands squeeze white around the Flock 28. I aim right between his shoulder blades as he walks to the rear of the van. Right between the shoulder blades, in the centre of his body, so that I'll still hit him if he makes a sudden movement. In my thoughts I tell him that he definitely shouldn't make any sudden movements.

I see Harry looking at me. A dark red flush is rising from his neck to his face. "What are you hanging around there for?"

"He's wearing trainers," I say.

"You. Wait!"

The youngster has a hand on the rear door handle. Harry gestures with his pistol for me to move to the back of the van as planned. In the meantime I'm wondering whether I need to intervene: never before have I seen someone from the organization in trainers. This is a situation Harry could misjudge.

The driver doesn't move. Only his eyes follow me, imperturbably cheerful. When I'm in position and the doors can be opened, Harry says, "Take off your shoes."

The youth glances back at me incredulously, but realizes he has no choice.

"Why are you wearing trainers?"

"They put them out for me, I wear them."

"They're organization shoes?"

"They're not mine . . . Wasn't I wearing them last time?" He kicks off the shoes and tosses them over carefully so that they land in front of Harry the right way up. "Maybe they can't afford leather anymore. Don't ask me."

Harry goes down on one knee and studies the trainers, which are relatively unadorned and undoubtedly a good bit cheaper than our shoes. He sticks one hand inside them, then checks the heels. In the end he points a spot on the heel out to me. I suspect it's the emblem, but I'm too far away to tell.

Humming, the youth levers his feet back into the shoes.

I wish it was over, that the doors would finally open, no matter what's in the back of the van.

Harry and I are kneeling on our left knees, hunched close to the ground in case there's a wild burst of gunfire. We'd never even register an exploding bomb; at this range there'd be nothing left of us. How I'm supposed to recognize one of the organization's random checks is a complete mystery.

I say, "Stop humming."

"Relax," the driver says and opens the doors, clicking them into position. I establish that I am still alive, my heart beating harder than ever. Harry stands up, the pistol at the end of his extended arms twitching as it follows the movement of his eyes wandering over the load.

After a while the driver asks, "May I?"

Harry's face is clammy with sweat. He nods, whereupon the youth starts whistling and bends over into the back of the van. I see plastic trays of various colours, each filled with a variety of foodstuffs. If there were more than just the two of us, our provisions would probably be in a tray too. The driver takes a cardboard box and fishes things out here and there. Finally he digs a carrier bag out from the side of the van and says out loud, "No crackers, but flour and yeast." Afterwards he stuffs the empty bag into his trouser pocket.

When he's put the bottled water on the ground too, Harry orders him back into the cab. He keeps him covered while I take off with the cardboard box. But after a few steps I feel the bottom collapsing from the weight. Without slowing down I lower the box and slide my hand forward, but can't prevent something from falling onto the concrete. I hear a dull bang with a sharp edge to it. Without looking back, I run to Number 22 and put the box in Mrs Privalova's garage. Panicking, Harry drags the bottled water back a couple of metres with one hand and screams, "Get out of here!"

Noise and light erupt again in all their intensity, unpleasantly familiar now and already less overwhelming. This time they accompany the departure of menace, their uproar dominated by the promise of peace and quiet.

11

When my eyes are used to the semi-darkness of the basement, I see Harry taking cover behind the water. All his tension has drained away, his limp arm is resting on the bottles, pointing at the entrance.

Not a shot fired. A success.

Between us, on the ground, there is a dark spot. Still shaken by the events, I don't have the energy to wonder what it could be. For the time being, I can only register its existence: a dark spot. I stay where I am, waiting for Harry to turn around and notice it. Then a strange smell reaches my nose, wavering, teasing. I feel like my legs are about to buckle after all when I suddenly realize that I am smelling strawberries. This knowledge is unbearable. I am drawn over to the spot. My cheekbones tingle and saliva starts gushing into my mouth.

Harry must have smelt it too. Without a word of consultation but almost simultaneously, we squat down on either side of the spot and stare in astonishment at the deep-red substance with the odd shard of glass sticking up out of it.

"I smell strawberries."

"Let's stay calm," Harry says.

I don't understand why he's keeping his hand on his pistol.

"Get the spoon. I'll wait for you. Promise."

Walking to the room, I try to work out how long we've been here and how long it is since we've tasted sugar. I can't think straight, my brain refuses to be distracted from the prospect ahead. I find the teaspoon, the only spoon we have, stained brown and seldom, if ever, used. I run back with it.

"I fished some of the glass out." He's licked the pieces off or used his finger to remove the jam: they're lying neatly together next to his feet like the well-gnawed bones of a roast chicken. "That's all," Harry says. "Just the glass."

Squatting opposite Harry once again, I ask, "How are we going to do this?" I mean, should we spoon the jam into another jar and save it for sandwiches? How much shall we eat a day? One spoonful, a spoonful each? They're questions we need to consider, but I can't put them into words right now because of the constant murmuring in my head.

Harry carefully scoops up some of the pulp with the teaspoon and raises it to my lips, presumably as compensation for what he's already enjoyed off the glass. The moment the strawberry jam is in my mouth, I forget the danger of glass splinters, push my tongue up against the roof of my mouth and gulp it down. My mouth falls open as if shocked into numbness, there's too much taste, I have to get rid of some of it. Like an overheated dog, I pant strawberry and sugar. Euphoria is already ringing through my veins as Harry takes some for himself. He looks me straight in the eye. We know what the other is feeling.

He scoops up another spoonful. Mine again.

Almost as a ritual, united in a sacred silence, we eat it all. A spoonful for Harry, a spoonful for me. The enormous basement disappears in its own emptiness. We have no trouble fending off the question of how the driver got his hands on jam. The very last mouthfuls, scraped together, contain dust and dirt from the concrete floor, but the grit doesn't spoil it at all. It goes down easily with the sugary jelly and is completely tasteless.

12

As if sitting around a campfire, we slump on our backsides and stare at the spot on the concrete, which now really has become a spot. Daydreaming. Moved to reverie by the pleasant glow of the sugar. Feeling mild about our situation, although it hasn't changed. I am so sated that I keep my thoughts about the possibility of there being more jam in the cardboard box in Mrs Privalova's garage to myself for a good five minutes before confiding in Harry.

"You think so?"

We scramble to our feet.

Wouldn't it be fantastic to be able to eat bread with jam every day for a couple of weeks? After what's just happened it doesn't even seem like an insane longing.

Harry folds back the lid of the box and starts pulling things out. I see the familiar tins of corned beef appear in the half-light, boxes of chicken stock cubes, flour, yeast. It's still possible. As long as he's bending over the box, it's still possible. It will happen without any transition. Harry will straighten his back while casually handing me a jar and saying, "Here. Cherry."

Harry shakes his head.

He runs his hand around the four corners one last time. "No razor blades again either," he says.

Rubbing and picking at our beards, which we trim fortnightly with a paring knife, we finally stroll back to the bottled water. We don't say it out loud. If we say it out loud the chance of a second miracle will disappear in a flash. Or do we keep silent because we don't want to admit to each other that we still have hope, completely irrational hope?

We circle the bottled water, acting as if it's about the water, as if we're inspecting the new provisions. In full harmony with this pretence, we don't let our disappointment show.

Suddenly Harry's face lights up. He asks whether I noticed. I'm staggered. Have I missed something? I'm about to inspect the water again, when Harry says, "The guard didn't come."

13

I nudge the float in the cistern. The water level rises and a few seconds later the whistling stops. I click the cover back on and take a piss.

Hardly an hour after eating straight strawberry jam, my urine smells like liqueur. In the water, which has settled again, I detect a slow movement as if there really is a viscous fluid floating in it. I stand there breathing deeply for a moment, telling myself that I am drawing the volatile sugars into my lungs and introducing them into my bloodstream a second time.

The water gushes into the toilet bowl. Like always, I nudge the button back up with my finger. It's no great inconvenience, you can do it in a single movement. It stops the float from getting stuck, which causes the water to keep running and makes the whistling sound.

"It's very easy," I tell Harry after returning to the door to our room. He's slouched on the chair, legs relaxed and spread slightly. There is an unavoidable sense that, after this nerve-wracking day, nothing else can befall us.

I explain it to him, the way the button springs back when the toilet starts to flush. But not entirely, probably because of the friction of the float against the inside wall of the cylinder. "A slight upwards push of your finger," I conclude, "easily helps the button to override that friction."

Harry struggles to put astonishment and approval in his expression. He taps his forehead a couple of times. "I'll make sure of it, Michel."

"Thank you, Harry."

14

A long column of gleaming black limousines passes the building; I start counting as a reflex. They're driving cautiously, not in any hurry. A funeral procession. Or is it a parade? The weather is exceptionally radiant. Standing as I am at the basement entrance, below street level and looking up through the open gate at the street, I can only see the car windows. The pure, fresh air tingles in my lungs. I'm too greedy and succumb to a fit of coughing. I don't hear myself coughing; I experience the contractions in my gut and the rasping in my throat, the pressure in my skull. I don't see any other buildings or people on the street. I don't hear any other cars. I don't hear anything at all. If I concentrate hard, I perceive the silence that has been twisted into my ears like cotton wool.

Standing on the edge of outside and inside, I feel the prohibition, the commanding presence of the mental borderline. In the same instant I realize that I am able to interpret my dream even while dreaming it, which explains my lack of fear. It seems I can even intervene in my dream at will. For instance, long before the end of the procession I know that there are thirty-nine cars, forty minus one. Whether I am the cause of this or am simply anticipating the total because I understand my dream, it doesn't really matter. Fully conscious now of the nature of the event, I see no good reason for remaining in the gateway.

The moment I take a step, extending a foot beyond the limits of the building, I feel a heaviness in my toes, my foot, my leg. As if I am entering another atmosphere with different air pressure, different natural laws and a different specific gravity for the human body. But that doesn't cut off any of my possibilities because everything in this atmosphere is subject to the same forces. We are on an equal footing.

I adjust to the conditions quickly. If I take my time, I can even run. The cars are proceeding as slowly as ever, more slowly in fact, because I am now nearing the rear bumper of the last vehicle. The weather really is radiant and I can see virtually nothing through the side window. There is no doubt about it; someone is sitting on the back seat. I know from my reflection that I am screaming. I think I am screaming with joy.

15

We eat around midday, when virtually all guards take their dinner break, but also because, with corned beef on hand, we find it impossible to wait until evening.

The air of the storage room is tinged by the new provisions. Despite the strong metallic smell that coats the inside of my mouth and reminds me of when I was a boy and accepted a dare to put my tongue on the two poles of a battery, the association with salted meat is overpowering and stimulates my appetite.

Under Harry's watchful eye, I use the key to roll back the thin metal lid, then cut the corned beef and arrange it sparingly on the bread. There is a festive gleam to the meat.

We eat calmly. We eat politely. Although Harry casts the odd exploratory glance into the darkness around the sides of the basement now and then, we are, for the duration of this meal, first and foremost people who are eating. Just as the whole city, as I imagine it, is populated in this moment by people who, in one way or another, are focussing their attention on their midday meal.

16

I think back on Claudia.

Claudia is in the service of the Olano family. Head of the kitchen. It's around 2.00 p.m. when the signal sounds and Harry and I turn our heads towards the lift.

The service lift signal is easy to recognize. All of the lifts give a signal upon reaching the desired floor. For starters, the service lift is louder; that seems directly related to its intensive use. What's more, the signals of the residents' and visitors' lifts are subtler, styled as it were to the taste and presumed intellect of the users. Modest, too. Compared to the rather matter-of-fact sound of the service lift.

Claudia has a gigantic body, curvaceous and relatively firm. She walks towards us holding a plate covered with an upside-down soup bowl. Some people might claim she waddles, but that's an optical illusion. What they see is the inertia of the mass her hips push up with each step. According to Claudia her parents named her after a film star from the distant past, when they still showed films in cinemas. She says we have to share the meal equally. We eat a kind of poultry we don't know and can't picture at all; it is unbelievably flavoursome. Ever since Chanel, the Olanos' lapdog, choked to death on a sugar cube, Claudia has arranged the leftovers on a staff plate. She wouldn't give the hot dinners the organization delivers to us daily to the pigs. Her parents have a farm in the north of her home country with a smokehouse for the hams.

We let Claudia sit on the chair. She asks our opinion. That hint of tarragon, it's not too strong, is it? Her eyes are the centre of any place in which Claudia is located. She has eyes that show pent-up jubilation and speak of a desire no-one can quench, which shouldn't be unleashed for that very reason. Claudia is beautiful to look at, even when she's depressed. She says that Mrs Olano has had a hard life and sometimes that impedes her contact with the staff. I eat poultry prepared by Claudia. Harry has already finished his share. I chew slowly and at length, out of politeness. At times Claudia watches my mouth as I chew, as if that mouth will reveal what I really think about the food. I look at her eyes, which are looking at my mouth.

We don't ask about her parents: whether they're still alive, for instance, or if she ever hears from them. Harry says that her father must be as proud as punch. A daughter – that's every father's dream. In service with the Olanos, in this building. A father could do worse. I ask Harry if he has kids. He shakes his head. He doesn't want kids, not in this world. By that he means the world in which he's a guard. He says that real guards shouldn't have daughters. You can't put yourself through something like that.

17

Today it's Harry's turn: he wipes the inside of the tin of corned beef clean with a piece of bread, soaking up the last bit of taste. When the bread is saturated with his saliva, he swallows it. We stay sitting for a moment on opposite sides of the bunkroom door. Then Harry walks all the way to the crusher in the narrow space between Garages 34 and 35 and tosses in the tin. The impact is painful. Not so much the uppercut of piercing decibels, as the meaning of the sound. Harry comes back smiling. He rubs his stomach and opens his mouth to say, "They can't take that away from us now."

18

I think of Arthur.

Arthur extends his arm: a well-filled blue dustcoat sleeve with a clenched fist at the end. His other hand points to its length and gestures that the walls are at least twice as thick. He was in service with the Duprez family for years, three streets away. He saw the building rise. Now he works for the Poborskis. He suspects that the bottom layers have even thicker walls, but on the thirty-ninth floor he knows exactly. He's quiet for a moment looking at the yardstick he's holding out for us. He says that the apartment has window seats like they used to have in fortresses and castles.

He grabs the two bin bags by their knotted tops. Piss off, I think, piss off! But Arthur just stands there, knees bent, stinking rubbish in each hand, as if he feels like he's forgotten something and is dredging through his memory. Why does he come to chat with us first before putting the bags in the crusher? Doesn't he notice the stench anymore? Has he always been at the bottom of the household ladder, where stench comes in many varieties, and has he gradually come to cherish those varieties as the peculiarities of his simple life?

Does he have a bad back?

I hope the bags don't leak, not a drop. That concentrate of rot and decay could stink for days, nestling into our room, where it's safe because of the lack of circulation. It will creep into our bedding and uniforms and when we start to think it's gone, it will be because the stench has taken possession of us in our sleep.

Finally Arthur says that the building won't collapse in a hurry. No, he's certain of that. Not with walls like these . . . He lifts the bags up from the floor. There are no traces left on the concrete. It's Arthur who told us that the building doesn't have any rubbish chutes: they're too dangerous, they'd be throwing the door open to biochemical terror. According to Arthur, rubbish chutes are a thing of the past. In older buildings they're sealing them up. He lugs the bags to the crusher, disappearing around the corner. We hear them flop down one after the other. After a short pause the motor turns on, building up the hydraulic pressure. When the maximum has been achieved, the motor turns off and the press starts moving. Deep in the container, almost simultaneously, we hear the bags pop like two balloons.

Arthur tells us that they lie full-length on the window seats and stare out. He undoes his dustcoat to arrange the panels neatly one over the other, then pulls the belt tight. They look out over the city like Roman emperors, with delicacies from all over the world in arm's reach. He's seen it with his own eyes, at least once. The window seat in the second living area is without a doubt Mr and Mrs Poborski's favourite spot. He says they made their fortune from insulating covers to use on ski slopes and glaciers in the summer. Without the Poborskis, Arthur claims, there would be no ski resorts left anywhere.

19

I wipe my plate clean with a piece of bread, clearly winning Claudia's approval. I praise her deer-calf stew. Particularly tasty. She smiles. Mr Olano enjoyed it too. He instructed the butler to call Claudia to the dining room so that he could compliment her personally. She says he's charming; she loves his big, warm hands. How does she know those hands are warm? Do the Olanos shake hands with their staff? It sounds unlikely to me.

Mr Olano is no stranger to the staff's living quarters. The five-star service was included in the exorbitant purchase price of his luxury apartment and he interprets that service in the broadest sense. Without knocking, he opens her bedroom door. It is very quiet, but vague noises from the bowels of the building still reach these rooms. The night light in the hall reflects in Claudia's eyes, she's lying on her side. Mr Olano calmly closes the door. He sits down on the side of the bed. Only after a while does he lay a hand on her hip, which rises up high under the sheet. A big, warm hand that gently explores her body, then moves her hand to his crotch. It doesn't take long, especially when he feels her other hand, which has found its own way. This is all Mr Olano requires. He touches her cheek for a moment and disappears.

But Claudia doesn't look at all as if she's let something slip or as if her words were meant to make me guess a secret. Perhaps she assumes that his hands are warm because he has a good character. In her world the two things go together. Maybe she dreams of one day feeling his hands on her hip in the darkness of her room, while he sits on the side of her bed and gently whispers her name. In her dream his hands are always warm.

20

The entrance gate starts to move. Harry and I move over to the residents' lift and assume the appropriate stance: feet apart, hands behind our backs. Although we serve the residents, we don't take orders from them.

It's Mr Glorieux's Aston Martin. He is accompanied by his daughter, her blonde hair catching the light behind the flat windscreen. The gate has now closed again. Vehicles have to wait a full minute in the sally port between the street gate and the building before the entrance gate opens.

A servant, a friendly youth who rarely stops to talk, steps out of the service lift. He assumes a pose that is scarcely different to our own. He is wearing a white shirt and a black waistcoat over black trousers.

The deep growl of the eight-cylinder engine creeps closer, a predator that can surge forward with all its power in the blink of an eye. The car stops and the servant opens the door for Mr Glorieux's daughter. She doesn't deign to look at him. The over-sized sunglasses on the top of her head are keeping her curls under control. In his brown leather pilot's jacket, Mr Glorieux walks around the back of the car and says, "Thank you, Ben." The servant nods and climbs in behind the wheel. With that same controlled growl, the Aston Martin creeps off to its cage,

Garage 14. When the lift doors slide open almost silently, Mr Glorieux lays a gallant hand on his daughter's lower back and says, "Gentlemen."

21

Arthur leans against the wall with one outstretched arm. He says that Mr Glorieux was one of the founders. That the plan to sell luxury apartments with the service of a five-star hotel was his. There was clearly a market for it, because all forty floors were sold before the derelict factory on the site had even been demolished. A spinning mill the city had been ignoring for years. Red brick, of all things. Trees growing up through the roof.

He thinks back on it with evident pleasure. He is a twelve-year-old boy whiling away countless afternoons on the factory grounds. His secret spot is under the roof on a weathered rafter that looks out over everything, where he rules like a king and smokes cigarettes like his father. He lures a girl here. She walks through the weeds on long, pale legs. Her name is Els. It takes hours before she lets him steal a kiss. In the very spot where the three of us are now standing.

Arthur tells the story of the body and the colony of cats. That the body of a toddler was once found here, or what was left of it, because at the end there were 163 cats living on the factory grounds. Not one adult cat was unscathed, they all bore the marks of furious battles: sockets where eyes had been clawed out, scars where ears had been ripped or bitten off, bald spots and suppurating wounds. Despite that, the neighbourhood always stuck up for the colony, especially when Mr Glorieux displayed interest in the land and began developing his plans. Petition followed petition, there were demonstrations, the factory gate was picketed, a brick went through a stained-glass window at the town hall. Not long afterwards they found what the cats had left of the toddler's body.

Arthur asks if we've ever heard the cries of a female cat on heat. He looks at Harry, then at me. "Just like a toddler," he says. "A toddler having a terrible nightmare." He says nobody in the neighbourhood slept well after that.

Silently Arthur raises his open arms as if to point out Mr Glorieux's building, as if to say that life can take strange turns. That a dead toddler can sometimes lead to something like this.

22

Mrs Privalova steps out of the lift on her assistant's arm. She inclines her grey head. It's a greeting, we know that, even though she doesn't speak or look in our direction. She is in her early nineties. Her assistant is a balding man with pink, full cheeks. Taking small steps, he goes to Garage 22. Mrs Privalova stands motionless on the short runner in front of the lift, leaning on her walking stick. She is festooned with antique jewellery and a sable stole. From the corner of my eye, I study her profile, which shows indomitability more than anything else. This willpower must be at the basis of her wealth. It is the willpower of the victor.

Then the inevitable happens. It happens every time. How terrible must it be for Mrs Privalova to suffer from flatulence? An ailment that announces its presence over and over. Her elderly body is no longer able to resist. What can she do except ignore it, pretending that the escaping gas isn't making the weirdest noises, as if her sphincter has degenerated into a fold of skin flapping lazily in the wind.

Harry and I look at her assistant as indomitably as Mrs Privalova: he is not very skilful with the Bentley and invariably forgets to shut the garage door. I'm standing closest to her and take shallow breaths, only admitting the air that is already in my nose out of respect for this woman. Presuming, as I do, that she would find any greater intimacy unbearable.

23

Mrs Privalova has just left when the signal for the residents' lift sounds again. The lift has been programmed to ensure that the residents are never forced into each other's company: it always completes a journey before answering the next call. It is extremely rare for one resident to immediately follow another. They could bump into each other in the basement.

Mr Van der Burg-Zethoven has a weekend bag with him. His fiancée is carrying their hairless cat, a hideous creature wearing a black leather collar set with gems. He walks to his garage, some ten metres from the lift, too impatient, apparently, to wait for assistance. They only arrived from their country estate yesterday. Their faces are grey with seriousness, or from the unusually early hour. A death in the family, thinks Harry.

But the couple, coincidentally or otherwise, turn out to be the harbingers of a flurry of activity among the residents. Harry and I count ten exactly who leave with luggage in the course of the day. Perhaps an important event is taking place in their circle – a premiere, the presentation of a prize, an anniversary or a farewell – and later, in some other city, they will all be guests at the same gala event, where they will recognize each other in the crowd on the dance floor as owners in the same building and start to talk, settling on some obvious subject of conversation, exchanging experiences, assessing and desiring the other's husband or wife, agreeing to see each other again sometime soon.

24

It's the depths of the night. Harry is sound asleep when I hear the signal for the residents' lift. For a moment I think I must have dozed off and am now dreaming that I'm sitting on the chair alone and hearing the signal for the residents' lift because I have heard it so many times today. But I am awake. Quietly I tell myself that I am awake and I clearly hear my own words.

Mr De Bontridder is wearing casual clothes I have never seen before. In this nondescript get-up, without the three-piece suits in which he leads a fabulously successful software company, he looks like an ordinary family man who has decided that tonight's the night to do a flit.

He comes up to me, talking as if he's obliged to answer the question he reads in my eyes. He is agitated: maybe he took something to stay awake and overdid it. He tells me a muddled story about information he's considered, parameters, reports he's been following closely, all day now. The input is steady, the calculations precise, the reliability has never been higher, the margin of error is negligible. A man like him can't stay blind. No-one can stay blind, no-one, make no mistake about that.

I watch his mouth opening and closing to the rhythm of the words, so far it all makes sense. But I don't get any further; beyond this point I seem to be lost in someone else's dream. I still experience the physical presence of all that surrounds me. I am in the middle of a stream of air issuing constantly from Mr De Bontridder's body. I am sure of that much. I can mainly smell leek, but also fish. Salmon, I think.

At this hour, it's only natural that I lend a hand. After he has fetched the Mercedes coupé, I load his luggage into the boot. The car is decades old but magnificently designed and, now that I finally have a chance, I can't resist the temptation to run my hand over its coldly gleaming silver curves while Mr De Bontridder, sitting at the wheel, talks into his telephone in a hoarse voice. Not much later the familiar signal sounds, the lift door opens with a sigh and Mrs De Bontridder dives into the passenger seat as if it's raining cats and dogs.

25

The next residents appear early in the morning. We're on our feet all day in a basement that's as busy as a train station. Almost no-one pays us any attention. Today we're a royal guard, constantly at attention, unable to be distracted from our official protocol.

Only Mr Olano shakes our hands late in the afternoon before

climbing in next to his chauffeur. A handshake accompanied by a solemn nod and "See you later." Although it's definitely not small or cold, his hand is neither particularly large nor particularly warm. His politeness, however, is most peculiar. Has Claudia told him about us in the darkness of her room? Has he ended up developing a soft spot for the two men in the basement who guarantee his security?

Peace returns in the evening.

Harry shakes his head. He's worked here longer than me and never experienced this before. There's nothing unusual about fluctuations in the occupancy rate: all of the owners have multiple residences at their disposal. But an exodus like the last few days', no, he can't remember anything comparable. According to his count there is only one resident left in the building. He doesn't know his name as he only goes out sporadically. A strange, withdrawn character in his early thirties, who keeps his head shaved and always wears black. Harry couldn't point out the staff who serve him either, not if they were standing right in front of his nose.

26

The signal for the service lift, after three days without any sign of life. A group of staff – presumably they all serve the same family – step out of the lift. They're in high spirits. The men laugh as one, teasing the women, who are made up and have let their hair down, tossing it over their shoulders or softly pushing back their curls. Their leave has started. They greet us casually and we give a cursory greeting in reply. Not one of them disengages from the group. Here, in the building, they stay close together as if lassoed with an invisible rope, walking as one unit towards the entrance gate and the outside world, where it seems to be quiet and where it is very likely that their relationships with each other will change rapidly.

Before the after-image of the daylight has faded from our retinas, the next carefree group emerges from the lift. The staff are paid not by the families, but by the building; it's only logical that they should get temporary leave during the residents' absence. Gradually Harry and I discern the composition of the groups. We can definitely point out the *chefs de cuisine* and the chambermaids. We nudge each other, nod at this or that stranger and immediately agree with each other.

Even Claudia, in the end, doesn't step outside her familiar circle of equals. She blows us a kiss. She waves. She tells us we mustn't misbehave, no matter what.

She looks back twice.

27

At the first bang we both drop to the floor, pitch-darkness is tossed over us like a blanket like a net, and we're caught, swearing, pointing our guns in all directions. At the second bang, which follows the first like an echo, the emergency lighting turns on. It's only after a few minutes that the tubes light up more than their own covers and the basement starts to reappear as a collection of shadowy patches.

Harry checks the entrance while I walk to our room. The two screens of the video monitoring system are dead; the cameras are aimed at the sally port between the entrance gate and the street gate. On closer examination, the screens are receiving electricity but no signal. The light bulb in our room is still on too.

Harry comes back, not having noticed anything unusual. He says he can't hear any voices or rumbling engines, nothing.

We spend the first few hours waiting anxiously, walking countless inspection rounds. It's strange that the cameras are no longer emitting a signal, though perhaps they are and it's just not reaching the screens. A short circuit somewhere that's partially cut the electricity supply. We look for a simple explanation.

We adjust to the darkness, which gives us the impression that the emergency lighting is increasing in strength. We see everything as clearly as before. Nothing has changed. After a brief consultation, we decide that at night, as usual, we will each take five hours' sleep in turn.

28

Two days later we watch with drawn pistols while the entrance gate opens. We understand why a day has been skipped when the young driver explains that the organization will no longer be providing hot dinners. He hardly looks at us, he's in a hurry, there's a dark sweat stain on the collar of his blue shirt as he informs us that from now on we will be receiving varied rations. He makes it sound like a simple policy decision, an extremely awkward one as far as he's concerned, because now he's got a lot more work to do on delivery days. Although he's been in the basement every day for the last few months, he shows no surprise at the emergency lighting. As if we have silently agreed that every one of us needs to adjust to the situation.

29

Harry rubs his stomach cheerfully. "They can't take that away from us now, Michel.' Sighing, he sits down on the chair next to the door. Dinner's over. Our intestines will digest the bread and the canned meat, absorbing the nutrients and concentrating the waste. The taste – that delighted our mouths so much that we swallowed too quickly – will fade away and be replaced by the taste of our own empty mouths. The taste of the instrument.

Ten minutes later we're walking next to each other. We follow the perimeter of the basement, hardly cutting any corners, keeping our hands behind our backs. The jam stain in the middle of the concrete floor has turned from dark-red to a brownish colour. After completing our inspection round several times in succession, it's as if, instead of guarding the basement entrance, we are now guarding the stain, circling it like sheepdogs to keep it neatly in position. Just past Garage 22, the closest to the stain, I spot a lazy fly rising up from it. It's the kind of fly that always seems to fly in squares. At least, it always does corners, never curves. It must have got in yesterday when the gate opened. I hope it doesn't lay eggs, that the traces of sugar left in the stain don't convince it to lay eggs. I feel an itch under my cap. Maybe it will come and land on my face in the night to probe the corners of my mouth with its proboscis, hungry and angry because there's nothing left in the stain. Maybe it will dare to venture between my slightly parted lips to eat from my teeth.

While striding along with Harry, it occurs to me that catching the fly now would be relatively simple. It doesn't rise higher than fifty centimetres or deviate more than a metre from the spot. The fly too seems to be guarding the stain.

I don't think Harry's noticed it. It's obvious that we can't afford to get wound up about a fly; that would be ridiculous. But at night when I am the first to go to bed, the temptation to check the room carefully is irresistible. All things considered, it's only a minor inconvenience.

I don't find any flies. Harry, who is sitting outside the door close to the chink, will have to suffice as a deterrent. I clean my teeth with my index finger, after first dipping it in a glass of bottled water.

The calendar is hanging from a nail in the corner and forms a diptych with the mirror above the washbasin on the other wall. The front shows all twelve months in two columns of greatly reduced reproductions of the inside pages. The Tengmalm's owl above October is a blur within a blur. Twelve endangered bird species, possibly already extinct. The cross I add before getting into bed is the second cross on this date. The double crosses stretch back four or five months. Harry started it, the day we got our first rations. A day to remember, he said.

30

Harry can't sit still while talking about the guard. He jumps up and straightens his jacket and tie as he starts to pace, a few steps left, a few steps right.

"It can only mean one thing . . ." He stops and points at my chest. "How long ago did the organization announce the guard?"

We both know the answer to the day, but I've been to university, so I'm better at that kind of thing.

I've sat down on the chair and stretched my legs, extending my toes as far as I can. The pleasure that starts in my muscles buzzes through my body and dims at the top of my skull. It's only after hesitating that I say, peering into space, "Six resupplies."

"Six resupplies ago, Michel. Six." Harry starts moving again. "Six resupplies: that's a very long time. And no message to the contrary in the meantime. If you think it through, systematically, it can only mean one thing."

I nod in agreement. When he delays the pronouncement of his conclusion, I say it for him, with appropriate pride. "It must mean," I say, "that we're doing an exceptional job."

Now it's Harry's turn to nod, at length. "Everything's going smoothly. No difficulties, no disturbing incidents. In all that time not a single intruder has dared to make an attempt! We haven't relaxed our grip. We've kept our eyes on the entrance every second. We've always maintained control. Given the nature of this building, that is quite an achievement." At those last words,

Harry lowers his voice and turns abruptly towards the empty space in the middle of the basement, head hunched down between his shoulders, hand on holster. But I've been keeping a sharp eye on everything.

He is rarely guilty of such inattention. Talking with your back to the open area could be fatal. You can't hear anything except your own voice and at the same time you're blocking your partner's view.

Harry recognizes the irony of the situation, slipping up while summarizing our record of service. His smile soon changes into a small but urgent warning to me. Did I see how fast it can happen?

"A formidable achievement," he continues finally. "Because hidden away like this, we can't possibly gauge the degree of danger. It has evidently become so large or unpredictable that the organization considers it necessary to station three guards here instead of two. Our continuing to take care of business is something they can't fail to notice, Michel. As long as they keep the reinforcements in reserve, we should see that as a favourable sign. A very favourable sign. Recognition."

31

I peer through the crack to the side of the entrance gate with my left eye first, then my right. I can't see any difference. The patch of night sky around the silhouette of the bare treetop is always uniformly dark. I can't make out any glow, no reflected flames in the cloud cover, no gradations of light.

Is the city dark and quiet? Or does the crack look out in the other direction, away from the city? When they brought me to this building they led me inside too quickly for me to get my bearings. Am I looking in the direction the wind is blowing from, carrying the silence of the countryside? I press my nose up against the crack. The cold draught seems to make the metallic smell of the groove even stronger.

I continue my round.

The authorities have declared a curfew: anyone who ventures out onto the street at night will be shot without warning. The snipers use silencers so as not to sow panic. The authorities have issued sheets of thick paper to black out the windows like in old-style wars. Is an air raid alarm about to go off? Is it possible that the endless silence will suddenly be shattered by an old-fashioned air raid alarm? How big is the chance of that happening while I'm thinking of it? No bigger than when I'm not thinking of it.

I stand still and listen.

32

It seems unlikely to me that the fly will ever find the crack and escape from the basement. Unless a bright light shines outside for an extended period, as bright as a spotlight aimed at the opening. The fly will starve to death. The rubbish crushers are hermetically sealed: the empty tins we throw in have been wiped clean with a piece of bread. There can't be any nutritional value left in the jam stain by now. Harry and I drop crumbs when we eat, but how could the fly find those crumbs? Inconspicuous crumbs which are as good as odourless in a basement that must be enormous to a fly. It must have landed on the floor somewhere to patiently await its death. It is no longer capable of flight. It isn't in our room. It's not there when I go to sleep and it's not there when I wake up. I look down at the floor constantly, searching for black spots on the concrete. I hope to find it, so I can squash it underfoot.

33

Harry says he finds it hard to believe. He says enough time has passed now to thoroughly train a new guard, no doubt about it. He stares ahead and, lost in thought, gently shakes his head. We're sitting either side of the bunkroom door, Harry on the chair, me on the stool. We could sit on the side of my bed with the door wide open to give us a good view of the basement. We could sit on the soft mattress. Obviously, we don't.

"The organization would never announce a guard if they didn't have one available," Harry says. "That's simply impossible."

"Extremely unlikely," I admit.

"They had someone ready," Harry says. "We have to face facts. Due to developments outside, the organization decided that there should be three of us on this job. They have, for the time being, reversed that decision because we're coping better than expected. Two of us are doing a job which they thought required three guards. Think about it, Michel."

"As long as we keep it up," I say.

"We have to keep it up," Harry says. "Do you think that jam came out of nowhere? You don't think it was a gift, do you? That jam was earmarked for the elite. The elite's rations include jam. Take it from me. Would you like to be able to eat strawberry jam on your bread every day? I know I would."

34

We drive through unfamiliar streets, passing extremely tall buildings now and then. Towers of shiny new glass, decorated with fleecy clouds. The gate on the street is already rolling back over its track as we stop. A sign announces that this is private property and a prohibited area. There is also a warning in various languages and a simple illustration pointing out the lethal, high-voltage wires above the thick yellow line three metres up from ground level. The two bottom languages must be Chinese and Arabic. We stop on a sloping drive just inside the gate and the driver sticks his hand in a scanner, rubs a card over a reader and types in a code. He then aims an infrared key at the top right-hand corner of an immense concrete gate. I'm nervous, my carotid artery is throbbing against the stiff collar of my new shirt. This is it, I think, as we drive into the gaping darkness. This is my last chance to make something of my life.

Standing in front of the car is a man who has been waiting for us; his features appear as the gate closes again. He is strongly built, his uniform fits him like a glove and looks as new as mine, though that's impossible. At first I can hardly believe it's the same uniform. I look at the breast pocket, the emblem, the lapel, the buttons. I look at his cap. Now I understand the odd regulations concerning the angle of our cap. That decision was made with this man in mind. It is not in the least bit ridiculous.

The driver hands me two meals and leaves. Carrying the thermos boxes as a gift to show I come in peace, I approach him, put them down on the floor between us and hold out a hand. There is no prescribed way for two guards to greet each other and I fall back on elementary politeness. He shakes my hand and tells me he's called Harry.

He has a strange accent from the north of the province. He comes from a family of farmers, pioneers, but those days are over now. Bob and Jimmy, his brothers, are guards too. He says security is in their blood, they have a talent for it, their father is a veteran. It's possible that the farming was going downhill; I don't ask. Maybe it was a logical progression after having to go to more and more drastic lengths to protect their land and livestock for ever-decreasing profits. Or is it more straightforward and have these men become guards out of conviction? Harry has light-blue eyes; I suspect that women find him attractive. He is younger than me, about four years. The skin of his square face is taut and clear. He has the bulging jaw muscles of a cow or a sheep. He comes over as extremely self-confident; I'm inclined to believe him.

He gives me a tour of the basement. We step into our room together, making it seem even smaller. He turns the tap on and then off again. He shows me the bottom bunk, which is made up perfectly. He keeps quiet about my predecessor. Has he given up? Was he discharged from service? Or did something happen to him during an incident? Is there a tacit agreement not to talk about such things? Because it would bring bad luck? Because it's disrespectful? Or do I just need to ask the question for it to be answered?

He explains the daily routine. He tells me about the residents, their idiosyncrasies, their cars, their children. He introduces me to the staff. Gradually I win his confidence. His face relaxes. We exchange stories. I believe there is a lot he can teach me. I am attentive.

35

"A hundred times bigger," Harry says. His eyes seek out the perimeter of the basement as if to verify that he has the correct proportion. He almost always uses a factor of one hundred, occasionally resorting to "more than a hundred times".

In half an hour I'll go to bed. Harry's voice sounds softer than in the daytime. We drank a thin stock and ate some bread and now tiredness has struck. My biorhythm is getting too regular. We would be wise to reverse the sleeping order to break the pattern.

"There's really no comparison to our situation," Harry continues. "Here we only have a single entrance to the building. One of those big country estates can be attacked on all sides and that makes it a lot more vulnerable. The kind of fencing plays a major role, true, but fencing never comes with a guarantee that nobody's going to get over the top or tunnel under it."

He sticks out his chin and gives the hair on his throat a good scratch. I point my rifle almost straight up and pull the trigger without hesitating. My shoulder jolts and the masked figure on top of the fence is lifted a couple of metres. The now motionless body falls as a dead weight. The thud on the ground is followed a couple of seconds later by a soft rustling as the mist of blood and pulp that was blown high into the sky rains down on the grass.

"A property like that is in the middle of a rolling landscape with magnificent trees, so you don't always have a clear view. Sometimes the boundaries of the property run straight through thick vegetation. But it still makes sense for the residents to withdraw to their villas and mansions and stay there for so long; they're protected by the elite. Some units are fifteen men strong. Together they're a well-oiled machine that never falters. They don't hire ordinary guards, you have to be at the very peak of the profession to even get considered. The owners want value for money and that's understandable. Even the simplest tasks aren't entrusted to just anyone. The chain is as strong as its weakest link."

Harry's account is enthusiastic. He tells me about it as if it's the first time I've asked him about the elite. His words fascinate me more than ever. They are old and slightly the worse for wear, but the story they tell could soon be our reality.

36

Harry says that they are exceptional guards, every last one of them. That's why positions almost never come up. He asks if I understand that properly. They almost never lose anyone. He shrugs. They're simply very difficult to eliminate. What's more, we mustn't forget there's virtually nobody who feels up to confronting them. You'd have to be pretty crazy, says Harry. But if it does happen, some commando or other trying to intrude upon the defences, our colleagues have the very best weapons and equipment at their disposal, including, obviously, a lot of high-tech gear. Lasers and thermographic cameras, for instance. Night-vision goggles are part of their standard kit. He tells me to stop and picture it. From an objective point of view their lives are more dangerous, true, their minefield is more densely sown as it were, but compared to the elite, we, Harry and I, are crossing ours blindfold. He grips the lapel of his blue jacket and shows it to me. Stressing his words, he asks me if I know what kind of suits the elite wear. He tells me the story about the suits that are made in three layers. It's a kind of diving suit, skin tight. The top layer is waterproof, the bottom layer registers body functions. The middle layer contains S.T.F., a fluid that immediately changes into an impenetrable shield when pierced by a bullet or sharp object.

37

"But that doesn't mean we don't stand a chance. Don't worry, O.K.?"

The door is ajar. I start to undress, slipping a coat hanger into my jacket and hanging it up on one of the three hooks on the wall. My shirt follows on the same hook. I hold my trousers up by the folded legs and lay them and my tie neatly under my mattress. I wonder how you hang up one of the elite's liquid suits.

"Our chances are actually very good. The organization has shown its trust. Our efforts haven't gone unnoticed. You and me,

Michel, we're a good team. We don't shirk our responsibilities. In all this time, the organization hasn't heard from us once. That still means something. That's quite an achievement. And considering the dangerous conditions outside, the demand for the elite will only increase. The demand always goes up."

I wash my face and rub my teeth with my index finger, scratching at the plaque near my gums in an attempt to remove it. Some of the plaque is calcified, I can never get the surface properly smooth. I hope the elite are provided with toothbrushes. It seems highly unlikely that they wouldn't be regularly kitted out with new brushes. With hard bristles, hopefully, the hardest bristles you can get, ones that scrape and polish. And toothpaste. I try to summon up a memory of the taste of toothpaste. It helps if I look at my old toothbrush, a fossil on the side of the washbasin. The nylon bristles have been pushed out in all directions, unravelling into bunches of fine pointy threads. It helps, even though this object cannot possibly be called a toothbrush anymore. Without prior knowledge, no-one would guess its purpose.

38

"It's possible that one of them eventually decides to call it a day. I admit, it rarely happens, but that's not the same as never. We have to pin our hopes on something like that, Michel, a coward pulling out and making room for a real guard. That's our chance of being liberated from this basement."

Although I dozed off the moment my head touched the pillow, my sinking consciousness crashes into his words, boulders of the here and now. They block the passage, forcing me back. I open my eyes but lie there motionless, pretending I'm still asleep.

Harry is keeping watch on the chair. "The way we keep the situation here under control," he says after a long pause, "is actually our training for the elite. You couldn't come up with better training. It's impossible to simulate. How could any training situation simulate what we have to achieve day after day, completely independently, with a minimum of facilities and equipment? Honestly, I wouldn't be surprised if our replacements, three of them that is, are ready and waiting right now to take over from us. Lying on their bunks and twiddling their thumbs. Like us, they're nervously awaiting orders. I wouldn't be surprised if we have to pack our gear during the next resupply and get taken straight to headquarters. Instructor Perec will be there to meet us. The old blowhard won't have changed a bit. Maybe he's died in the meantime, who knows? Who cares?"

I hear him scratching his beard – on his neck – because he's stopped talking. He stretches the skin and uses all of his fingers. The ends of the curls grow back into his skin, irritating and itching. The hairs lie flat and escape my attempts to trim them with the paring knife. If I tried to cut them off shorter I'd nick his throat. Shaving him wet doesn't work either. The knife is blunt and slides over his beard. Sometimes I pick at a loop with the point of the knife, but it's not sharp enough either; I need a needle. Very occasionally I do hook one and then I can very carefully pull back the ingrown hair. They're always centimetres long and watching them slowly appear is repulsive and fascinating at once. I don't tell Harry about my idea that one of those hairs might finally reach his oral cavity and poke into the bottom of his tongue or find a crack in his larynx and cause a constant tickle in his throat he can't get rid of no matter how much he coughs.

"In the mess, we'll be able to sit down right away for a full meal. With any luck there'll be fried potatoes on the menu and a slab of fresh meat with gravy. The dessert will be pie or custard. We'll take both back to our table, nobody will give a damn. While we're eating, they'll brief us about what's in store for us. There'll be no time to lose. They'll want us on the job as soon as possible. In less than a week we'll be ready. The training will be technical more than anything else, making sure we know how to handle the expensive gear the elite has coming out of their ears. Then we'll go out into the fresh air, Michel. Blue and green as far as the eye can see. It will take quite some getting used to. We'll walk around without masks; the local readings will prove it's safe. Fresh air in abundance. We'll get drunk on oxygen. We'll be guarding Mr Van der Burg-Zethoven's villa. You and me, Michel, we'll walk around his white villa side by side and guard his fiancée and her hairless pussycat. They're worth every penny, that's what Mr Van der Burg-Zethoven will think when he opens the curtains in the morning after a refreshing night's sleep and sees guards, armed to the teeth, patrolling his English garden. No-one, he thinks, will try to lay a finger on my fiancée and her hairless pussy, I'll make sure of that. And us walking rounds, you and me, under a bright sky. Nothing escapes us, and when a cloud drifts in front of the sun we can look in through the big windows and see his fiancée stretched out on the sofa while she slowly strokes her completely hairless pussy. We're happy, Michel, to see her so relaxed. Her blind faith raises our spirits. After all, we work long hours. We never relax our concentration. We're always on edge. That's part of our profession. And the elite's medicine chests really have it all. Every morning there's Modafinil to keep us alert and get the best performance out of our brain cells. Creatine to bulk us up, because in extreme situations we have to be able to take out intruders with our bare hands. If we're exhausted but can't get any decent sleep because of the stress, we get Temazepam. And so it goes. Whatever you need. Paradise on earth. Our ability, Michel, to effortlessly keep our heads above water in primitive circumstances like these is something that is discussed with awe by all ranks. Take it from me."

39

Perec doesn't look back, he gestures with one shoulder that I have to follow him. We stick close to the front of a tall building, our shoulders sliding along the smooth stone facade. I can't hear any other sound in the whole city, not anywhere. There must have been a gas attack – not a single pigeon in the sky – but it's strange that we can breathe without masks. How long ago did the attack take place? I can't see any bodies lying around, no people who threw themselves to the ground in the hope of finding some oxygen, salvation, while their features were eaten away, disappearing into the holes in their skull. And what are we doing in town? Why aren't we on site somewhere, why aren't we at our post? Guards stay at their post, they don't patrol the city. What's come over Ferec? I should kill him. I could easily kill him. I only have to aim my pistol and fire a bullet into the back of his head and no more Perec. He's as vulnerable as any human being. I concentrate on the spot where his spinal column joins his skull. I can see the curve of the bone very clearly through his bristly hair. I could press the barrel against the base and aim up at his forehead to maximize the bullet's trajectory through his brain. I could do it; no-one would suspect me. But I don't. I don't shoot him dead. I spare Perec's life out of self-preservation and follow him closely. It seems to be the only thing I'm still capable of doing. Without Perec, I would slump down against the smooth facade and sit on the ground next to his body, waiting for whatever was going to happen to me.

40

I can only have slept about an hour: my body is sluggish, as if paralysed head to toe. As heavy as a walrus, I lie on my stomach. The left side of my face is pressed against the pillow. Something has woken me. It takes superhuman effort for me to move my right eyelid. The semi-darkness in the room is different, disrupted. I realize that I am looking at a big shadow on the wall. The outline is hazy, but I recognize the shape of Harry's cap. He's standing at the foot of the bed, out of sight. He's standing there looking at me and stays like that for a while. Then he takes off his cap and lays it on the table. He hangs his jacket up on a hook without a coat hanger. I feel his weight pressing down the side of the mattress. His hand is on the other side of my body and he's leaning on it, the way a parent sits on a child's bed before giving it a goodnight kiss or drawing a cross on its forehead with a thumb.

Harry pulls the blanket back and joins me on the bed. Behind my back I hear him spitting on his hand, twice; sometimes he does it three times. I grip the metal bedframe tight, it's icy cold, my hands go numb. I notice a vague smell of bark. Harry plants his right arm immediately in front of my face, a solid pillar. The play of the dim light emphasizes the veins that crawl over the back of his hand like fat worms heading for his fingertips. Instinct tells them where to go. Like Harry. No thinking required. You just follow the chosen path to the end.

In my mind's eye a light shines on a portrait of my parents, a framed photo that doesn't exist, which I compose while looking at it. My mother is in a lady's suit with her knees turned aside and her ankles crossed elegantly, sitting on the edge of a French armchair: carved wood, curved legs, lion heads. Her hands are resting on her lap, relaxed but self-assured. Half-hidden behind her is the unassuming figure of my father: a servant charged with sliding up the chair. They didn't endow me with any distinct talents. They gave me their kind support. They increased my confusion. With infinite patience, they sketched panoramic views when I needed coordinates and precise orders.

41

We clean our pistols daily. Every morning after the second inspection round. We never do it simultaneously. We sit either side of the bunkroom door. As Harry clicks in the safety catch of his Flock 28, my arms are stretched out towards the entrance with my finger curled around the trigger. In a flash the fifteen cartridges are in his jacket pocket and the pistol is disassembled on a cloth on his lap. Slide, barrel with chamber, recoil spring guide. The black, steel-reinforced polymer frame. The magazine tube, the magazine spring, the feeder. I recognize all of the parts in the corner of my eye. In my mind I speak their names out loud, as if they're essential information I must never forget, words I have to be able to retrieve even when semi-conscious, long after I've forgotten my own name.

Harry only does what's strictly necessary. Neither of us says a word, the procedure demands absolute concentration. Having your pistol in pieces on your lap is an extremely vulnerable position. But it is incontrovertible that we also love the ritual and the reassurance of understanding the technical side of the tool we use and, given our profession, rely on to protect our lives.

In less than two minutes, Harry has carefully cleaned the barrel and tested the sear and the firing-pin spring. A dry, insignificant click. And then another, in full accordance with the regulations: the joy of twice pulling the trigger. Then the rapid succession of precisely fitting locks and engagements that turn the inconsequential pieces of metal into a deadly weapon.

42

I can hear it clearly. The sound has been absent for a month; I recognize it instantly. The toilet is to the left of the storeroom, our bunkroom to the right. When we're not using the toilet, we always leave the door ajar to let it air. I can hear the whistling to about midway through the basement, beyond that the sound is too vague and I'm no longer sure whether I'm actually hearing it or just imagining it. Like a month ago, the sound is just below the hum of the emergency lighting. I imagine it as taut, extremely thin gauze. Other noises pass through it freely.

43

Perhaps Harry's hearing isn't as good at those frequencies. "A whistling sound?"

"Do you hear the lighting, the hum of the fluorescent tubes? It's just under that."

Harry looks at the light fittings for a while. He tilts his head to a ridiculous angle, horizontal, as if to literally catch the whistling sound in his ear as it falls from above.

"No, I can't hear a thing."

"Nothing at all?"

"I hear the emergency lighting."

"Not the whistling?"

"No whistling. I don't hear any whistling."

"Just under the lighting."

He shakes his head. "I don't hear it."

We continue our round: the hems of our trousers tapping against our polished shoes; the heavy material of our uniforms rustling and rubbing as our legs cross. Underfoot, now and then, the grating of a stone, stowaways smuggled into the building in the tread of expensive tyres. Harry slows and stops. Frowning, he looks at me.

"Do you hear other noises too?"

"What do you mean?"

"Whistling sounds. Have they been bothering you long?"

I search his face for a clue, reading the lines and folds around his mouth, nose and eyes. I take my time, giving myself two seconds, three, four if necessary, to discover that he's having me on. That he's simply been slack and neglected to push the button back up, so that the float jams and the water keeps trickling. That he can hear it just as well as I can, the running water, and now I notice that the sound is as clear here, on the opposite side of the basement, as it was over there. As if the toilet has been moved behind my back to Garage 5. If I couldn't see where I am with my own two eyes, I would swear I was standing next to the toilet.

44

In the end we completed the round, marching all the way back from Garage 5 in silence. I heard the whistling constantly, but didn't ask Harry about it again.

I push the toilet door wide open, ignoring what I experience as an increase in volume, ignoring what my ears tell me. I want certainty, confirmation. I mustn't exclude the possibility that the never-ending exposure to almost constant silence has affected my hearing.

I ask Harry to come in. With a shocked expression he joins me in the cubicle that isn't really big enough for two people. I am already kneeling in front of the toilet bowl. I ask him to watch over my shoulder while I press the tip of my finger against the inside of the enamel where the water gushes down when you

60

flush. To my great relief I see and feel the initially invisible trickle build up and find new paths on either side of my fingertip.

"The toilet's leaking," says Harry.

45

I turn the key in the lock of the storeroom door through two full circles and see at a glance that the ammunition is all there with every box in place, just as they were eight hours ago. I count per shelf and do the multiplications in my head. Fifteen times three is forty-five boxes. Flat and rectangular, long sides against each other. The Winchester cowboy spurs his horse, never getting any closer to himself. I check each box separately, starting with the weight, although that of course can never be a valid criterion. Behind the flap, the cartridges stand in tight lines, immaculate and gleaming like polished jewels. Our most valuable possession.

I like being in this room. I take my time. The room appears to have been created by chance in the lost space between three supporting elements, but now derives its importance from the function it has been given, the ammunition on the shelves, the food and bottled water against the wall opposite. Necessities for the protection of the building.

I think of Harry and how he assigned a function to his life at an early age, deriving importance from it. The way he owns our modest uniform and how well it fits him. How he is driven by the goal of becoming an elite security guard. He has never been lost space in a dark corner of a basement where there is no longer so much as a breath of wind to disturb the accumulated dust.

I count all of the cartridges in all of the boxes. Time has no hold over them, they are patient, they look exactly the same as the first time I counted them. Winchester, 9mm Luger (Parabellum). And like that first time, the final qualification reminds me of the Latin adage, *Si vis pacem, para bellum.* If you want peace, prepare for war.

46

At the door of our room I inform Harry of the results of my inspection. We pull out our Flock 28s. In turn, we silently count the contents of the cartridge clip. After I have given Harry a nod, he repeats the total from the storeroom out loud and says, "Plus two times fifteen."

We sit down and eat bread I baked this morning. I added ingredients in the correct proportions and turned on the machine; it's questionable whether that justifies my claim of having baked bread. Sometimes I feel like it's not enough. There's something missing, without which the bread, although delicious, is not real bread at all but an outstanding imitation. Harry couldn't care less. He tears off chunks and stuffs them in his mouth in one go. It's remarkable how he always manages to find room to turn it over and chew it up without opening his mouth.

Afterwards he tells the story of Claudia and the frangipane. Chewing has brought back memories, or is it his craving for sugar? Or something else I can't even imagine? The story dates from an increasingly distant past, but sounds like it might just as easily have happened yesterday, this morning or an hour ago. Claudia just stepped back into the lift.

Harry is relaxed, seated, legs spread slightly. He touches his tongue with the tip of one finger and collects three crumbs that have fallen on his trousers. He nibbles them between his incisors while continuing the story, which happened while I was asleep in bed. It is a drawn-out anecdote that ends with a misunderstanding Harry finds extremely amusing. Today he forgets to mention the buckled patent-leather shoes. And although it's a minor detail, he gets Mr Colet and Mr Toussaint mixed up again; they both drove a white car.

47

Mr Van der Burg-Zethoven's fiancée lies stretched out between high walls, Italian marble extending up to the cornices. Lukewarm water trickles from a gold tap and the heady smell of cherry blossom wafts through the bathroom. She rises up from the froth, which slowly slides off her body. She dries herself with a thick towel, thoughtfully, as if dabbing a wound. She rubs lotions into her skin and plucks her eyebrows. She files her toenails and varnishes them pale pink. It is only at the very end of her toilet that she steps into a dress, lifting the bands up over her round shoulders.

It is a morning full of hope, the sky is blue. She sits down and informs the servant that she would like to drink grapefruit juice for breakfast, sweetened with half an orange. And afterwards, as usual, a large cup of coffee topped with a thin layer of frothed milk. She uses a silver teaspoon to scoop strawberry jam onto crusty bread. She rests her elbow on the mahogany tabletop and holds the slice of bread up to her supple lips. Catharina's weight is suddenly on her lap; immediately she starts to purr and settle down.

Outside the sunlight is sparkling on the leaves of hedges, shrubs and trees, on the blades of grass in the beds. Even on the helmets of the patrol. The two guards hold their dark weapons diagonally across their chests as they walk side by side across the lawn. They almost never stick to the paths, a sign in part of how reliable they are.

Mr Van der Burg-Zethoven's fiancée is imperturbable; she carries on with the life she has always led, unbothered by the heightened security measures. She enjoys watching the guards, who have become, in a sense, her possessions, part of the villa's furnishings, things she can gaze upon unhindered and even touch, should she so desire. They are like the works of art hung on the walls and mounted on plinths. Their secrets stir her imagination.

48

I imprint the days in my memory. After waking – before washing and dressing – I look at the date on the cover of the calendar. Then I look inside for the day of the week. As it's last year's calendar, I add one day. Wednesday is Thursday. A year is made up of fifty-two weeks and one day. Of course, the calculation is imprecise, the surplus is added every four years. Next year we reach that stage: I'll have to add two extra days and three from 29 February. Wednesday on the calendar will be Saturday in reality.

Around noon, forgetfulness sets in. If I succeed at this point in summoning up the correct day, I remember it until it's time for me to go to bed and dispatch it to the past with a cross. Much more often, I get my memories of the countless concentrated moments standing in front of the calendar mixed up. Understandably, because they always take place in the same circumstances and in the same light, week after week. I manage better when I'm sleeping before Harry. When I'm sleeping after him and wake up slowly in his presence, I say, fairly regularly, the name of the day out loud. "It's Thursday today." Harry never reacts. My days have been noted. I am often sure that I have remembered the day correctly only to discover in the evening that it's Thursday again tomorrow. Or already Saturday. Memories of mistakes are especially confusing.

49

Mr Van der Burg-Zethoven's fiancée is appalled by the sight of the guards. Their constantly increasing numbers, their heavily armed presence: it ruins her breakfast. It ruins the garden, the villa, the art collection. It rubs her nose in the facts. Everything around her is compromised because no-one can say what's in store for her. The guards owe their existence to potential danger and therefore personify it. Their being there evokes the horror that could strike her, in whichever form, a horror that would end everything that is familiar to her, what she sees as her life, the person she is.

She orders the servant to activate the sunshade.

Perhaps she would prefer to not hire any guards at all, telling herself that none are needed, that the state of grace in which she lives will go on forever. After all, nothing has happened for so long. Gradually she would forget the threat, bolstering the illusion. Not one secure second would be spoilt again. Until the day they've all been used up.

50

The last tin of corned beef. We've stretched it out so thriftily over several meals that the last bit tastes strange, already slightly tainted. We no longer eat the meat on bread. I lay the precious cube on my tongue and smear it against the roof of my mouth. The saliva starts to flow and mixes with the salty taste. I wait for a long time, until my taste buds are saturated, then swallow tiny gulp after tiny gulp until my mouth is empty. Harry eats the meat a little faster, but with comparable attention. We've wiped the tin out with bread several times. We've pushed the tips of our tongues into the corners. Harry has put the tin on the floor next to the leg of the chair. It sits there like a memento, no longer smelling even slightly like something edible.

51

I could just snap that he's damn right. Kneeling in front of the toilet bowl, I keep my fingertip on the enamel. The toilet is leaking and together we stare at the stream of water splitting into two. It's as if I'm constantly pointing at him, the transgressor, forcing him to repent. He apologizes. He won't be so remiss again. He spontaneously promises to always push the button up with his finger. He swears it on his father's grave. Because he understands better than anyone my need to keep the environment clear and tidy so that my thoughts can settle into their familiar groove and relax a little. That's all. I'm not asking for anything else and Harry realizes that. That's why he bows his head, ashamed of his careless negligence. I stand up, brush the dust off my knees and tell him it's O.K. No, he says quietly, it's not O.K. As he's leaving the toilet, I briefly lay a hand on his shoulder. We're a unit; we take each other into account. We depend on each other. He watches over my freedom, I watch over his. That allows us to relax and sleep at night. In this world we are each other's only security. We differ, that's true, but those differences make our unit more complete; the organization has paid careful attention to that. We are like a left eye and a right eye. Together we see depth.

52

I study the bare tree through the crack to the side of the entrance gate. Over the whole crown there are a dozen dry leaves still hanging, each at the tip of a branch in the very place where they are most exposed to the wind. I don't know if this is a sign. The old fear of a nuclear disaster takes hold of Harry.

"Have a smell." He nudges me and stares intently at my nose as I stick it in the crack. I doubt that radioactive fallout can possibly manifest itself as a smell. I feel like a canary in a coal mine. I breathe in reluctantly and instantly distinguish stone and iron, smells which become ordinary even during that first inhalation and cannot in any way be linked to danger. After three or four breaths, I'm convinced that there's nothing else to smell. I look back at the tree. I look at the section of wall tapering up to street level, over which, once again and for weeks now, the strange, dark-black shadow of an elongated, triangular object outside our field of vision has been slowly sliding; it will disappear again in spring.

"If it was a bomb," I say, "an explosion, then it must have happened a long way away. No more than a couple of nuclear warheads, maybe a targeted strike against a city on the south coast. A large-scale attack would have caused a cloud of dust that blocked out the sun."

Harry leans on the entrance gate. "The groundwater's contaminated," he mumbles to himself. "The tree has been defoliated through the groundwater, through the roots. It's nothing to do with the season. That's why the leaves on the end of the branches have been spared the longest."

A nuclear disaster or a small-scale atomic attack would explain a lot, first of all the silence in the city: a mass evacuation or wholesale flight to escape airborne death. Is it possible to clear an entire city, or better, is it possible to mute all of a city's noises? Will the thick walls and our subterranean location protect us from radiation? I concentrate hard on Arthur; snippets of his monologues about the construction of the building echo in my mind, but not once do I hear him talking about lead. Or is that something that has been taken for granted for ages? Including lead lining in the walls of extremely expensive new buildings? Is that why we never get to see the remaining resident? Because there's no need for him to show himself? We've already determined that he must have an immense larder at his disposal.

I think of the driver, the young guy who, instead of appearing in uniform, showed up last time in a baggy blue pullover and trousers without a crease. I wonder if lead thread is woven into those garments, if that could be the explanation. Was he decked out in a new kind of chain mail?

Will Harry and I end up besieged by desperate mobs, repulsively mutilated, who attack slowly and with inhuman patience, scratching at the concrete for months on end with screwdrivers and knives until the groove disengages and they, with their combined strength, can push the entrance gate just far enough aside? Will we be able to maintain our mental health until the last moment, saving our fire until the enemy is in sight?

53

Harry bends over the basement floor plan, gripping the table tight as if he's about to lift it up and hurl it across the room in fury. I'm standing at the short end, at right angles to the plan. He doesn't agree with me. He says it would be a sign of weakness. What clearly disturbs him the most is not the nature of my question, but my having asked it at all. He can hardly believe I've asked a question like that, he's disillusioned. "Don't you think," he says after a while, without looking up, "that the organization will inform us when the organization considers it necessary to inform us?"

"We could just touch upon it in passing?"

"You want to exchange chit-chat with a punk like that?"

"I mean, we could ask him an innocent question or raise the subject without immediately exposing ourselves."

"You've gone mad. You do you realize that, don't you? Asking a subordinate for an explanation. Don't you understand? That would be risking everything we've built up so far. In all the time we've been posted here, the organization hasn't heard from us once, not once. For the organization we're a completely autonomous two-man unit that looks after itself and that's why we're on the verge of a well-earned promotion to the highest level you and I can ever attain. We're a two-man unit that knows what it has to do – guard this basement – and also knows what it's better off not doing – asking superfluous questions. And that's what you want to start doing in the middle of resupplying, during a standard situation, the only occasion on which we might possibly be subjected to one last test before the organization decides to transfer us to the elite. Just think about it, Michel. Think!"

He doesn't deign to look at me, he's deeply disappointed. It was an ill-considered suggestion. I look straight at Harry, waiting for him to glance in my direction so I can express my regret wordlessly. But he points at the map, at the entrance gate, and carries on where he left off. The hairs of his moustache are hanging down over his upper lip, the tips discoloured by the acidity of his saliva.

"So he comes in here. He'll open the gate and drive the van into the basement. You take up position at Garage 3, keeping him covered. I'll ask for his I.D. and a confirmation. When I give the signal, you walk to the rear of the van. The moment the driver opens the doors, we have to assess the situation."

"No time to talk," I add eagerly. "Each of us, separately, decides whether or not to open fire. But if one of the guards opens fire, the other joins in unconditionally."

"Dead right," Harry mumbles.

54

Resupplying is already four days late. We spend most of our time sitting down and staring vacantly at the empty basement. We've run out of flour and yeast and bottled water. To conserve our energy, we've decided to reduce the inspection rounds to a minimum; who knows how long we'll have to get by on our reserves.

We speak little. The hunger even weakens Harry's walnut smell, not that it makes him any less nervous. Now and then a drop of sweat runs over the black polymer of his Flock 28, which he constantly grips tight in his right hand, at most resting it briefly on his thigh. I don't tell him that he's burning up masses of valuable calories. We only give our shoes a slight rub, but still brush off our coats and trousers like always. We have postponed washing our shirts and underwear. Harry sits on the chair, I'm on the stool; I stick my pillow between my back and the wall.

Harry doesn't get to sleep at all in his five hours. Eyes wide open, he lies there listening to the inexhaustible silence. He is convinced we're being subjected to the ultimate test, that the time has come to show what we're made of and that, as a consequence, it's ridiculous to think that resupplying will happen in the daytime when we expect it. For myself, I keep my eyes open because I'm scared of dying in my sleep.

Halfway through the sixth day we decide to take up position on the chair and stool against the wall of Garage 4, in immediate, visible proximity to the entrance, while maintaining a clear view of the three lifts. All things considered, it seems more advisable. On the long journey over there we stop twice, resting on our loads to catch our breath.

55

Waiting for the entrance gate to click on: I imagine a woman in the middle of a bare, tiled hall, holding a crystal vase out in front of her. At some stage the vase must fall, that's the agreement, the scene's outcome . . . Endlessly, I see the vase descending through the air, which seems shocked by so much abrupt responsibility and is still trying to prevent its fall, while at the same time surrendering, withdrawing its hands as it were. Time and again, I see the lowest point of the vase approach the tiles and touch them. I watch as the vase's mass keeps moving, like a whale disappearing into water, a car crumpling against a wall, until its speed falters, the first resistance makes itself felt, the fracture lines branch through the crystal, creating shards, and finally cancelling out the shape of the vase. I see it again and again, time after time. Eventually I'm able to make out the high-pitched sound waves that sweep swiftly towards my head over the unmoving mirror of silence and break on my eardrums. It has long stopped hurting. I know what it sounds like, that's why it can't touch me. But the unending repetition is alienating. Is that what a falling vase really sounds like? I start to question the whole thing. Could this scene have another outcome? I watch closely. In my heart of hearts I believe that the vase will fall, but apparently not now, or now, or even now, not even within the foreseeable future; we learn that from experience, from time spent waiting. Perhaps that is the source of the confusion. I have time to study the woman and think of other possibilities and I think of them. While I am pondering this, the woman lets go, the vase falls, the sound hits me full on and completely unprepared; the entrance gate starts up.

56

We jump as if hit by a surge of electricity and immediately we're
ourselves again, no longer hungry, no longer sleepy. It turns out
to be night-time, as Harry predicted. After just a couple of steps
I get tangled in the beams of the headlights, apparently swinging
my arms around because I swipe Harry's head, his cap. He shoves
me and shouts over the racket, "Position!" His push was in the
right direction. Taking the source of the scorching light as my
point of reference, I quickly reach the spot near Garage 3 that I
have spent long hours staring at from my prison on the stool,
goaded by its terrible proximity. I spread my legs slightly, stretch
my arms out in front of me and aim my service weapon just above
the thundering engine, which is slowly approaching. Through
the soles of my feet I feel the massive weight of the gate descend
on the concrete. The engine turns off. My ears are ringing.

Gradually I regain control of my eyesight. The familiar
emblem on the bonnet, large, presumably designed to be recog-
nized from the sky. Again, spotless bodywork lavishly reflecting
the basement's frugal emergency lighting. The driver says, "Here
we are, then." He's lowered his window all the way down into
the door. It's only when he gets out of the van that I recognize
him. He's wearing the same clothes as last time: the blue pullover, trousers without creases, trainers. The clothes are loose on
his body, like normal clothes. He is tall and scarcely twenty. Does
the organization choose underprivileged, foolhardy youths to

work as drivers in the radioactive zone? Is his inflamed skin a first sign of contamination? Do they simply neglect to inform them about the conditions and the dangers? Is that the easiest and cheapest solution? I can't see any adjustments to the van. There's no oxygen tank mounted on the roof. It's an ordinary van.

"A sight for sore eyes," he says. "My good old buddies."

"Shut up," Harry says. "Papers. And fast."

The driver shows both passes.

"And who are 'we'?" Harry asks.

The youth casts a cool glance over one shoulder, then looks back at Harry, who still has his pistol trained on him from behind the van. "God knows *who* you are, but you look pretty hungry."

Harry comes very close to losing his temper. "You said, 'Here we are, then.' Who are 'we'?"

The driver grinned. "Me and me mate." He raps on the side of the van.

For us, that rap is a punch in the face.

The guard.

Harry turns as white as a sheet.

I feel like my legs are about to buckle and force my knees back to lock them in place.

The driver raps on the van a second time and says, "We've had some wild adventures together."

The silence that follows is broken by the youth's nervous laugh. "Before you attack and eat me alive, I've got rations in the back. Do you hear me?" He waves both hands. "Can you understand me?"

"Who did you have those adventures with?"

"My friend here, made in Korea. Have I come at the wrong time?"

"You mean the van?" Harry asks.

75

The driver looks over his shoulder silently. I aim at the spot where his eyebrows meet.

"Answer!"

"Of course I mean the van."

Harry signals for me to join him at the rear of the van. As usual we take cover close to the ground. While the driver gets ready to open the doors, I see out of the corner of my eye that the barrel of Harry's pistol is shaking like a leaf. Get it over with, runs through my head. I'm exhausted, empty. I'm a shell. The idea of not shooting, of giving my assailant time to take aim so that one bullet will suffice, is almost overpowering. An irresistible prospect.

The doors swing open on oiled hinges, the driver clicks them into position – left, right – then takes a step back.

I'm alive.

And hungry again, more than ever.

57

From where I'm standing the load compartment looks empty. I study Harry's expression. He stands up and visually inspects the load.

"Everything in order, boss?" the driver asks.

As Harry nods, I stand up too. Before the youth bends into the back of the van, I catch a glimpse of the load. Not hard plastic trays in a range of colours, just one cardboard box accompanied by bottled water, stowed in a corner. The driver has to crawl into the load compartment to reach the ration.

The box is a good bit smaller than the previous one and exudes the smell of stale lavender. It once contained fabric softener, eight two-litre bottles.

Harry is almost beside himself with impatience but his hands stay glued to the Flock 28 while the driver, with growing reluctance, kneels to pull the bottled water back out of the depths. "Hurry up," Harry snaps, coupling his order with a poke with his foot just when the youth is at his most defenceless. "Take it easy," he says, remarkably unmoved. "I'm almost done."

Afterwards, leaning on his door, his right leg already in the cab, he looks us both in the eye by way of farewell. To me he seems much more mature all of a sudden. While dropping onto his seat, before slamming the door shut, we clearly hear him say the words, "Be glad I still bring you anything."

58

We're sitting next to the cardboard box, in front of Mrs Privalova's open garage, at a reassuring distance from the entrance gate, and neither of us is inclined to stand up and put an end to this party. For one and a half hours we've been sitting here as if in the company of an old mutual friend, who is telling us about long journeys, summoning up images of small harbours enclosed by steep mountainsides, sun-baked fishermen on strangely shaped boats who toss the morning's glittering catch onto the dock while the cool breeze rattles the rigging. There is a blissful peace on our faces. We have earned this, even though we wisely stopped after a quarter of an hour's gorging. Our initial regret about the lack of anything sweet, which evaporated at the sight of the tins Harry arranged around the box, now starts to nag again. Sugar would be a welcome change after the rich taste of fish in oil, but of course we don't complain. I saw my own overwhelming desire reflected in Harry's eyes as he tore open the first tin and shook the chunk of fish out onto his hand as if it was coming out of a baking tray and the sensuous golden-yellow oil ran down between his fingers. Fortunately our stomachs have shrunk and the deranged flurry passed quickly, before we did even more damage to our limited month's supply. We know what we have to do; we just don't feel like it. Everything has to go straight into the storeroom, under lock and key, we have to put an urgent end to our debauchery or face another period of devastating hunger. Harry leans back on his elbows, a pose people adopt on the beach, gazing out to sea. He says he could fall asleep just like that. If he closed his eyes for three seconds he'd be gone. I remind him that by rights I get to sleep first. He sniggers and agrees and says that, given that it's now early in the morning, I have the right to go to sleep first in approximately sixteen hours; we'd do better to come up with something else. He's in a playful mood and suggests that whoever makes it to the bunks first gets to sleep first. His words curl around between us before stopping and hanging motionless in the air over the cardboard box. Then, as if our fragile bodies have already made a full recovery from days and days of starvation, we scramble up and run to the door of the bunkroom, clawing at each other's arms and screaming with laughter.

59

An hour later, I'm baking bread. Harry is snoring as if he's faking it, his eyes resting deep in their dark sockets. Bread will alleviate our most pressing needs, delivering the desired volume to our stomachs. It would be better if we didn't open any more tins in the coming twenty-four hours. We have to battle the temptation with fire and sword. And after that, we need to reinstate our former iron discipline and keep ourselves going on a minimum of fuel. After the tyranny of blind hunger, I consider myself capable of living off the smell of baking bread alone.

60

I think of Claudia.

She's dozens of metres above our heads in the Olano family kitchen, which is equipped with everything a chef desires and where this bread maker, before the arrival of a newer model, once stood. Every lunch Claudia is the centre of a circle of braising, steaming and simmering, sautéing, hissing and spattering. The smells she brings to life cling to her, hanging onto her skirts like children, refusing to let go. After lunch the cheerful crew descend to our basement. A cloud that completely engulfs us, veiling the sharp-edged world.

61

We are sitting in our vests on either side of the door, which is ajar. The armholes hang loose under our arms. No matter how much liquid soap I use, the cotton stays grey without hot water. I've polished our shoes. The new shine keeps catching my eye. Our blue shirts are hanging upside-down to dry on the side of Harry's bed.

"Do you know what your brothers are guarding?"

"Apparently Jimmy's elite. An embassy. I heard something about it just before I got stationed here."

He slides his cap back to scratch his head as if he's about to launch into a complicated story, but doesn't elaborate. He uses both hands to put his cap back at the prescribed angle. His broad forearms are deathly pale with the occasional long curling hair here and there, ginger like his beard.

"And Bob?"

Harry shrugs. "Bob's Bob. He'll have blown away a few bad guys by now. It wouldn't surprise me."

I don't know why I brought up his brothers. Maybe because he told me about Bob and Jimmy himself when I started as a guard, about their special bond. And because that made their being posted to three different districts so peculiar. Were we subject to a special policy designed to protect families from multiple losses from a single incident? Or was it their own free choice? Thinking back on Harry's stories now, I realize that they were all set in their childhood, on the farm; I can't remember any others. Three young men in a hole up north. One beautiful, fickle girl would have been enough.

"No embassies for me," Harry says. "We're going to a villa. A white villa surrounded by gardens. You and me, Michel."

It's detectable, albeit with difficulty, the slight hesitation in his voice. The euphoria after the absence of the guard and the arrival of food seems to have ebbed a little. We are both being drawn back to the driver's last words, spoken as if he was exhaling them while moving towards his seat. As if, rather than being formulated, they were being forced up out of his chest by his rising diaphragm. They have put down roots, deep in our subconscious, and are now pushing up quickly towards the light.

62

We're doing a round when I break first and raise the subject of the resupply.

"That's right," Harry says. "The cardboard box was in the furthest corner . . ."

"Do you think he could have been keeping the rations hidden there? Out of sight of someone who happened to glance in through the windows?"

"Hidden? Then he would have thrown a blanket over it. The ration was right there in the back of the van. Why would he want to hide it?"

I shrug. "There weren't any other boxes in the load compartment."

"I noticed that."

We shuffle on for a few metres until Harry gradually picks up the pace and we're back at our normal tempo.

"We were the last address on his route," he says. "That's why the box and the water were right up the back."

Were we the last address? It was the dead of night.

"If we were the last post on his route," I say, "then it's strange that there weren't any empty trays in the back of the van. Trays he gets back when he makes a new delivery."

"Maybe they put everything straight into storage at other posts?"

I see four or five beaming guards in a storeroom. One stands at the trays, the others at the shelves. The first says the name of the provisions out loud, then tosses them to the right man. In a few minutes everything is in its place.

"Then the load compartment would be filled with the trays they've just emptied, surely?"

"True."

"He was eight days late," I say after a silence. "That's a long time."

"There could be numerous causes for that, Michel. Causes we can only guess at."

"We almost starved to death."

"We might not have been the only ones. Maybe we got off lightly. Maybe other places have suffered casualties."

"You think?"

"I don't know. The main thing is we're not dead. Understand? You and me, we're still alive."

I'm washing our socks, kneading the wet, black lump against the sloping sidewall of the washbasin. Harry comes up behind me. When I neither stop nor turn around, he sits down on my bed.

"The driver said, 'Be glad I still bring you anything.' What he meant was: *We* should be glad *he* still brings us anything. We should appreciate it. He meant: I've been racing around all day. I'm knackered. But I've still made it here with your provisions at this hour. And then you treat me like this. He must have been pissed off about me kicking him in the bum after such a long day. That's what I think. That explains his reaction."

"Maybe," I say, "but I didn't get the impression he was reacting out of anger. Plus, he didn't look knackered. He didn't look like he'd been working all day."

"Those guys are all front, Michel. Even when they're knackered. What were we like ourselves? Always ready with a smart answer. Never backing down."

I wring the water out of the lump cautiously, trying not to rip the old material. I hang the socks up on the side of Harry's bed. It will take hours for them to dry.

"His day's almost over," Harry says. "His second-to-last address is close to the depot and we're more or less on the way back to base. So he thinks, I'll unload the van first, then I won't have to drive all the way back later. That's why the van was already empty, except for our ration."

64

It's night. In these unchanging surroundings lit by emergency lighting, the days don't differ from the nights. But still my wristwatch and biology have the capacity to colour the hours, dividing the days into sections. It's night and I walk past the garages alone.

I keep my eyes peeled, but let my mind wander. I feel like Harry and I have overlooked something. If only the driver had stressed the most important part of his sentence. That's the problem. What, for instance, does it mean if he'd meant to say, "Be glad *I* still bring you anything?"

Should we be happy that he in particular has brought us these things? And what does that suggest? Does he mean that we already have another driver? That he's not the only driver on this route, and we should be glad that *he* is still bringing us something, because he knows the other driver isn't?

But maybe he wanted to say, "Be glad I *still* bring you anything."

Has something caused a cutback in resupplying? Has there been a significant reduction in the number of drivers available and should we be glad he still comes? Is he virtually alone because no-one else is willing to do the job? Because it's too dangerous? Is there a strike going on or has a mutiny broken out?

Or was his rash outburst that we should be glad that he still brings us *anything*? And should we conclude that daily necessities are in short supply, that there is an even more pressing shortage than the shortage which has been in force for so long now? And is that why he came at night, to avoid attracting attention? With a ration that was considerably smaller than the previous one? Is that why he came with just one ration, so that if he was robbed, he would only lose the one, and was that why it took him so long to resupply everyone?

I lean back on the entrance gate, close to the crack, the whirlpool in my head making me dizzy.

I hear a cyclist.

I hear a cyclist, no doubt about it! Every cell in my body stirs. The cyclist is coming from far away and headed in this direction. I recognize the sound as if he or she cycles past here every day, although I've pressed my ear against the crack countless times since the exodus of the residents and never heard anyone or anything. And now this, in this city, a cyclist, unmistakable. With each turn of the pedals, the chain scrapes over the chain guard, making an almost ringing sound, and when he or she is at the level of the entrance gate, I hear the groaning springs of what sounds like an old-fashioned bike seat, maybe a large one, a lady's seat. I press my face against the crack. Vaguely I make out the wall tapering up to the street with the shadow of the tree above it: nothing else. But still I am certain that he or she is not cycling on this side, but on the other side, against the normal direction of the traffic, or at least in the middle of the deserted street. I listen for perhaps a full minute, until the rattling dies away and only the hum of the lighting is left.

I have heard it so clearly, my perception of it has been so acute that when I turn back to face the basement, the image of the cyclist is branded on my retina.

65

He feels the tension in his thighs. His muscles are as hard as steel, not just when he's pushing down, but moving up now too. Tension that imperceptibly crosses the line to pain, at least where the bundles of muscle are attached to the knee joint, the spot that is taking the most stress because the bike is too small for someone his size and he never gets a chance to straighten his bent legs. The bike is the cause of his pain and this ride. They found it in an alley, a rusty lady's bike, an alley here in the neighbourhood, where they had no business being but still turned a profit, abandoned as if the thief had jumped off years ago and left it leaning against the wall, suddenly disinterested in his escape vehicle, dumping the evidence of his snatch and grab, a drug addict investigating his spoils next to the tilted bike, stashing money, credit cards, tablets and a mobile phone in his coat and tossing the rest up onto a roof where no-one will notice it and a suspicious stray cat will sniff it many months later before spraying it, day after day, so that years afterwards the new inhabitant of the building will pick it up between two fingers with even greater aversion, this stinking, weather-beaten object, after having pulled on rubber gloves first and, to spread his weight, crawling out over the old tarred roof on all fours, studying it carefully and, without turning, calling back to his wife at the window that he thinks it's not an animal after all but a handbag, he's as good as certain, and then he holds it over the side of the roof and lets it drop into the alley next to an old lady's bike. The alley on the edge of the neighbourhood that is now restricted access, on whose borders they linger at night, bored out of their skulls. Until one of them slips on something disgusting in the dark, maybe a dead cat, and knocks over a bike as he falls.

A bike. None of them have ridden a bike in years, bikes are for kids and boring adults. But tonight this bike is a stroke of luck, a gift from the gods. After a bit of fooling around, he's the one who suggests a suicide ride straight through the neighbourhood that is the subject of the wildest rumours, with the real reason for it having been declared off limits lost in everyone's memory. He should have kept his big mouth shut, he drew the short straw. The rattling chain drives him on, he swings his shoulders to push harder on the pedals. He has to go faster, faster. He feels naked to his bones. He's an easy target. What's he got himself into? Can the hair in his nostrils filter air? And what kind of microscopic germs will grip onto those hairs, his eyebrows, the inside of his ears? What will dissolve in the water on his eyes? Will the wind on the round surface drain it off towards his cheeks or push it back in the other direction? Entering his body through the tear ducts?

66

His muscles are on the point of snapping. All at once they will break free of his knees and whip back, curling up towards his abdomen. He's too big for this bike, but he had no choice. The only taxis in sight were already taken. He ran down the

pavement in a panic, crossed the street several times and frenet-
ically searched the memory of his telephone for numbers. The
shortest waiting time a taxi company could offer him was fifteen
minutes. In reality that meant at least half an hour, assuming
it was an experienced driver who knew the shortcuts in this
permanently clogged city, where a car could get up to twenty
kilometres an hour at most. He studied the drivers in the traffic
jam through their side windows, trying to make out a friendly
face behind the reflections of the neon-lit night, someone who
might listen to his pleas. Then he saw a bicycle leaning on the
fence of a small park, a remarkable sight. The days of casually
chaining bikes to rails, posts or trees are long gone. The old lady's
bike was leaning against the wrought-iron fence at quite an
angle, like someone who's suddenly been taken sick. He couldn't
see a chain or lock. There was nobody in the vicinity paying any
attention to the bike; people walked past it as if it was a beggar
or a street kid. When he focussed on it, it seemed to be located
in a parallel world that had nothing to do with the bored drivers
and indifferent pedestrians. A world in which they were pre-
destined to come together. He ran across the street, grabbed the
handlebars without stopping and jumped onto the wide seat.
Within the first five metres he felt the bike's abnormal resistance,
something wrong with the crankshaft. It wasn't that bad, but
he had a long way to go. The fear of getting totally exhausted
halfway and having to dump the bike against a fence somewhere
was not unfounded. Except he had no choice. Halfway would at
least be halfway. Mapping out the route in his mind's eye, he saw
the angular patch he'd have to cycle around. He only hesitated
a few seconds. Sweating and panting, he turned down the first
side street. He ignored the warnings, relatively bland symbols on
a prohibited entry sign. Fifty metres further along a bright light

flashed intermittently over similar signs, to which a blue rectangle with flashing electric letters had been added. He read,
Attention! Or, Warning! Or, Reminder! He jolted over street
markings and speed bumps. He passed immense signs with the
universal phrases in various languages, beacons in the night,
unpleasant gusts of hot air on his overheated face. No barriers.
A weathered plywood sentry box in the middle of the pavement
betrayed how temporary people had first estimated this problem
to be. No longer manned. According to article such and such
one enters the zone at one's own risk. Emergency services won't
come this far for anyone. Without thinking, he keeps pedalling,
turning into a long dark street flanked by tower blocks the street
that cuts straight through the zone and will get him to his wife
in a third of the time. She's in the delivery room, scared, it's all
happened very quickly. He has to be quick too, faster. He too has
to push his body to its limits. If he becomes one with his effort,
clenched from head to foot, an immense fist, his body will be
impenetrable The virus has dozed off, weakened, it can't keep
up with him. He feels the wind in his hair, he sees the metres
passing under his wheels. He won't tell his wife. He'll get there
in time to witness the birth of his son.

67

Harry and I have had a miraculous escape. In some fortuitous
way, this space has saved us from a painful death. Either that or
we have the dumb luck of simply being immune. The organization was prepared to sacrifice us to save the building from mass

looting, but the looters were terrified and never materialized. People outside of the protective ring don't know we're living in this basement. The remaining resident is sprawled on a carpet somewhere in his apartment, on a handmade Oriental carpet. Lying there untidily like a dropped handkerchief. The carpet has been completely ruined. The juices that have leaked out of his decomposing body have eaten away at the fibres. He is still dressed in black. Shoes, watch, glasses. We were mistaken about his staff: they, of course, left with the other domestics. He misjudged the situation. He stayed a day too long. He thought it would all blow over. He wanted to show how fearless he was. He wanted to stay with the precious heirlooms inhabited by the soul of his late lamented mother. He was penniless. He had nothing left, everything had been sold: land, thoroughbreds, shares, yacht. The apartment had been stripped. He had nowhere to go. He didn't know where to hide. He took a gamble. He preferred the risk of the virus to the certainty of shame.

68

I spend a full hour standing at the crack to listen to the city. I try to put the cyclist out of my mind so I can resume my inspection round. On the way to the bunkroom, I can't control myself; I cross the basement and march back to the entrance gate.

That night I only do half rounds.

In the nights that follow I put the stool next to the gate. Now and then I walk a short distance so that I can peek around the corner of Garage 1 at the lifts and our room. Most of the time I stand at the crack, swapping ears regularly; the draught is cold. I get a headache from concentrating so hard in an attempt to sift the slightest of sounds out of the silence. I hear what I think is the extra tension on my eardrums, or the murmur of my overheated brain. I am aware of the danger of hallucination. The silence is like a desert.

69

By breaking the silence the cyclist has confirmed it. He's locked it down. The sound of his passing was the turning of the key. There is no-one left in the city except an idiot on an old bike and two guards in a basement. Harry was wrong. There is no last resident left in the building; after all this time we would have picked up some sign of life. Everyone's gone, everyone has fled. The city wasn't evacuated, its inhabitants just ran for it. Harry, me and the mad cyclist have been left behind. No-one informed us. Just as some people predicted, a new kind of war has arrived – conveniently referred to as the New War. A war whose very existence is subject to question, no-one knowing whether it's already raging or yet to start. Something from a futuristic novel. The weapons and the wounds they cause, the objectives and which parties have set them are anybody's guess. And *that* is the chief characteristic of this world war. That's what makes everyone flee: the enemy is unknown.

We've slipped off the organization's radar. After a nuclear strike on the south coast they would have come to pick us up. After a bioterrorist attack they would have done everything in their power to lift the quarantine in this crucial part of the city as quickly as possible. Harry and I have been left behind. There is no longer anyone here for us to protect and no concrete threat to the building. Our ongoing posting here is an administrative oversight made by a commander who has cracked under the pressure. That's why we no longer hear anything from the organization – not because we're carrying on in silence and doing such an excellent job. That's why the guard doesn't show up. They've forgotten us.

The driver has secretly stockpiled tins in the warehouse. He's delivered them to us in cardboard boxes, not the usual hard plastic trays. He has tried to amuse us with jokes. Gradually it's been getting too risky for him and he decided to postpone resupplying us for a week, eight days, he decided to come at night. He was not particularly pleased with the way Harry goaded him, but he showed that he understood the reaction, he didn't get angry. And as for us, we can be glad he still brings anything.

70

After a long silence, Harry says that for starters he is quite capable of counting to forty. He speaks calmly. He says that if I had ever seen the last resident, I would understand why he's not the kind of person one casually overlooks. Particularly because he seldom shows himself. As there is no other exit, he would have needed to come past here during the exodus and Harry would have noticed him. He says, slightly louder, that the organization does not forget its guards. He keeps silent for a moment to give me an opportunity to recognize the absurdity of the inverse. He says that the delay in resupplying was either planned by the organization or a direct consequence of outside events. In both cases, a harsh trial for us. But we're not here for our enjoyment and I should know that. Lying in a hammock under a palm tree never got anyone into the elite.

71

I'm impressed by his ability to stay calm and his faith in the organization, which has revived in the few days since we've been resupplied and is once again irreproachable. He's also renewed his habit of dropping to the floor without warning every now and then to do fifteen push-ups. He again radiates the composure of a man who is living for a simple, unambiguous goal he has set himself or at least accepted. No longer questioning the existence it brings with it. His dedication seems rooted in wisdom.

72

I've only been at the post two or three weeks when Harry announces early one morning that the profession of guard is always undervalued. His claim comes out of nowhere. The building is bathed in calm; even the domestics, as I imagine them, are still sleeping peacefully in their narrow beds. His words dissipate in the air of the basement. I've imagined the whole thing. Then he asks, "But how much more credit do you get for building a house or driving a train?" I don't answer him. I know he's not expecting me to. He says that people demand something super-human from guards: do nothing, wait and stay alert. An almost impossible task. Repelling an attack is taken for granted. If nothing happens we seem superfluous, almost inconvenient. Idiots with side arms, that's what people take us for, interchangeable pawns. They – pointing up at the residents – don't have a clue. They think they're leading important lives, but they're just bubbles in the air and without us, they'd burst at the slightest resistance. This – pointing at the concrete between his feet – is the real world. "You and me," Harry says, "we're in it up to our knees."

73

"Hundred times the size," Harry says. "At least. More, I think. Anyway, it will be one of the most beautiful gardens you and I have ever walked around in. That's what I mean. Just magnificent. And you know what it is? The owners, they just look at it. At most they sit in a chair out on the terrace and look at their garden. As if you just look at your stunning wife and never kiss her or pinch her on the bum, let alone do it with her. That's what it's like in those circles. A garden is something to look at."

Harry digs the dirt out from under his fingernails with his thumbnail. A garden is something to look at. It doesn't sound like he's made that up on the spot.

"It's a question of days."

"Days?"

"It won't take much longer. A few days. Maybe a week."

We're standing left and right of the bunkroom door. We are both fully dressed. I've washed everything except our suits and caps, carefully soaking the ties, then letting them drip dry from the side of Harry's bed. I've tied knots in both of them, because when Harry puts his on from scratch he ends up with a rock-hard lump halfway up his throat. The last sheet is hung to dry over the chair and the stool, which we have set up in front of the residents' lift on our left.

"But we've just been resupplied."

"They could bring our replacements in between times too. There are three of them. That's a lot of people for a full van. Instead they could be part of a special deployment, together with other new guards, in a truck that covers the whole city."

"Wouldn't that be a little risky?"

"Why?"

"For the organization, I mean. A truck full of new guards. You could see that as precious cargo."

"They'll scout out the route first, Michel. The truck will be armoured and accompanied by elite troops."

"Do you think we'll get to leave straight away?"

"What would we stay here for? There's three of them."

"To clarify certain things. You know. The way things go here in the building."

"We jump on the truck and we don't look back. You hear me? I had to work it out for myself too. There was nobody here."

"Nobody?"

"No," Harry says. 'Nobody. I was the first. Two months later another guard joined me. The way it was actually meant to be from the start."

The question about the fate of my predecessor is on the tip of my tongue. I don't know if the silence that follows means he's waiting for my question or, inversely, that he doesn't want to talk about it.

"There's three of them," he says. "They're better trained than we were. The training keeps getting better. We don't owe them a thing, Michel, we've more than earned our promotion. We've served our time, so we shake hands politely, wish them luck and jump on the truck. Headed for a new life. You and me, in a fabulous garden somewhere. Trees, flowers, birds. Waking up to the chirping of sparrows, just like on the farm. But without the stench of pigs and cows, without the racket, without the drudgery. With any luck we'll be able to pick peaches, oranges and soft sweet pears straight from the trees. What are the owners going to do with all that fruit? Just eat it, they say. The juice runs down our chins. We're sitting out of the wind on a bench, having a little rest, turning our faces to the sun. Fresh air. Everything is green and blue. Enough to drive you mad."

74

"I think we'll be requisitioned."

Harry takes another large bite of the piece of bread he's holding. He keeps staring ahead into the dark corners of the basement, knowing he has my attention.

"By a resident," he says, nodding his head to swallow. "It goes against organization practice. The organization prefers an impersonal guard–client relationship. That's proved more favourable for both parties. In the long term, definitely. But these residents are extremely wealthy. If clients like them have a preference, if they make an explicit request, what's the organization going to do? You think they're going to give them a lecture on company policy?"

He rests the spout of the plastic bottle on his lower lip and lets the last bit of water glug into his half-open mouth. In a flash he's screwed the bottle up into a ball. Returning from the crusher, he paces to and fro for a while in front of the empty chair with his hands in his pockets.

"And what of it?" he says. "So what if the organization kicks up a fuss? So what if they politely but firmly inform the client that they alone decide who guards what, with all the accompanying explanations? A client like one of the residents in a building like this will just slide a few extra notes over the table, won't he? Simple."

75

Harry says he hopes Mrs Rosenthal won't requisition us. For five days now the requisition scenario has had us in its grip. Harry is in bed and still drowsy. It's 5.30 in the morning and he has only just woken, which makes his announcement about Mrs Rosenthal come across as the end of a nasty dream. The bunk-room door is ajar and I ask him through the crack if she was the elderly woman on the thirty-second floor. He says the Jewish bag lived on twelve and must have been around forty-five. A real face-ache, she'd never give you so much as a smile. He says I must know her son, a skinny little guy with an undersized hat and a patchy beard. A permanent grin on his stupid mug. Begging for a beating, according to Harry. He daydreamed about it often enough: whacking him over the head as if he was a naughty boy, just slapping him smack on the cheeks. After which the Jew would undoubtedly grin even more, now that he had tempted him into physical violence, which would almost certainly lead to Harry's dismissal. After which Harry would then punch him full in the face, smashing that big schnoz of his. He'd like to see him grin with blood all over his gob. It would make things a lot more bearable. A little later Harry says he wouldn't be surprised if Junior begged Mummy to requisition him specifically, as his plaything, in the sick hope of one day being worked over by him in reality. He probably can't keep his hands off his pee-pee just thinking about it. Yes, Harry says, that gets the little twerp hot alright, Sabbath or no Sabbath.

While getting dressed, he asks if Jews are allowed to keep dogs. He thinks it's the kind of thing I'd know. He says he's never seen a Jew with a dog. I think about his question. The combination of Jew and dog is hard to picture for me too, but I'm not sure why. I'm not even able to come up with a reason why the Jewish religion would prohibit the keeping of dogs. Harry says, either way, we should hope for a post where they don't have dogs. No matter how good you keep your eyes peeled on patrol, sooner or later you step on a turd and get to spend quarter of an hour scratching the orange shit out from the tread of your shoe. As depressing as it gets. If it's up to Harry, preferably no dogs. Anyway, despite their masters' claims to the contrary, dogs always stink.

76

The residents' names come and go. Day after day they visit us in the basement offering us panoramic views of fabulous gardens in which we can move freely, in which we can breathe and live freely, providing security under the very best of conditions. We've got plenty of choice.

Some names emanate an intoxicating perfume as if someone, hidden behind a pillar, presses an atomizer the moment the name is spoken. I've stopped going over to sniff the residents' lift; it was foolish to expect the door seal to smell of anything except, vaguely, rubber.

77

I try to explain that both Mr Toussaint and Mr Colet had white cars, but Harry won't listen. He thinks I'm trying to put him in his place. I clarify my position by saying that I'm not correcting him when he says that Mr Colet drove a white car. He's right. Mr Colet did have a white car, something American. But in the particular incident with the frangipane, although it's trivial, he actually means Mr Toussaint, not Mr Colet. Because Mr Toussaint also drove a big white car and that's probably why

Harry has switched the two men. After all, Mr Colet had nothing to do with Claudia. Harry says that Mr Colet definitely liked them plump, or women with a fat backside at least. But that is beside the point because Mr Colet didn't know Claudia from Adam. He just happened to also drive a white car. That's why Harry confuses Mr Colet and Mr Toussaint. And it is, by the way, Mr Toussaint, not Mr Colet, who is a distant relative of Mrs Olano, with whom Claudia was in service. Harry looks at me and says he can't believe it. He turns away and sulks in silence for a long time. I say that it's not important anyway. It's a detail, it doesn't matter. Then Harry says that I was asleep at the time. If I was asleep, how can I know whether it was Mr Colet or Mr Toussaint? I tell him that I still know Claudia. Claudia told me about it herself.

78

Harry swears that it was Mr Colet and wants that to be the last word on the subject; he quickens his pace, taking a slight lead. I leave it for now.

The discussion makes me think back on Mrs Rosenthal's son. Until recently I remembered the Jewish youth as a devout figure with an affable smile for all who crossed his path, regardless of creed, status or position. An odd creature, true, an adolescent with the air of an old man, something I put down to exceptional intelligence. But the way Harry described him was just as accurate. He could also have been a pernicious brat who got his kicks by grinning in people's faces to wind them up, especially those who served him and were, therefore, in a sense powerless.

It's happened several times in the past few days. Mr Schiffer's personal assistant for instance. I don't believe he suffered from a skin condition. I think he was an alcoholic and that Mr Schiffer turned a blind eye as long as he didn't shame their confidence or let it compromise his work. He was after all, I assume, an extremely correct, civilized and capable man. But his face was red from the booze.

It was as if I had insulted Harry personally.

Which made me doubt myself for a moment.

79

We're sitting on either side of the bunkroom door, silent. Suddenly I no longer have any idea what time it is or which part of the day we're up to. It has struck me out of the blue. I must have been deep in thought. I wrack my brains, but can't recall what I was thinking about so deeply, even though it was just a second ago. I try to reconstruct the hours, starting from the inspection rounds; their interchangeability doesn't help. I can't find anything concrete. Nothing that unmistakably locates me in the present, in this present. Then I think, disbelievingly and with mild self-contempt, of my watch. How could I have spent so long, second after second, not thinking of the watch that will give the correct time as long as my heart keeps beating?

Now that the solution is at hand, I postpone it a little. For the pleasure of it. As if I'm on an excursion in countryside that's full of surprises. I'll turn back soon. There's plenty of time.

I become aware of the absence of my body. How long have I been sitting in this position? I don't feel anything anymore, my body has gone completely numb. As a consequence, I have the idea that I can no longer move. Afraid of failing, I don't dare to simply try. My eyes roll easily in all directions and my eyelids blink like before; the rest seems anaesthetized or paralyzed. I concentrate on my feet, sending my thoughts down to them, scouts in search of a sign of life. I send them to my left foot first, forcing them to my little toe. I work systematically, from bottom to top. Arriving at my backside I encounter cold emptiness, as if I'm sitting on concrete instead of a wooden stool. In my lower back, which is leaning against the wall and bearing the weight of my relaxed upper body, I even discover pain, concealed in habituation.

I stay sitting in the same position, surrendering to a state of contemplation or detachment. In the corner of my eye I see Harry sitting motionless on the chair. I want to maintain this condition as long as possible, this complete quietude. But I know that eventually a word will be said, a superfluous word, that will make me jump out of my skin. It's inevitable. In one intense spasm all of my muscles will be called to order.

Is Harry thinking about his prediction? A good five weeks have passed since he claimed that we would be relieved within a week. Is he still thinking of the residents? They have almost disappeared from our conversations. Frequent use has robbed their names of their power. They have degenerated into abstractions, sequences of letters.

The smells faded away long ago.

During one of my night rounds I stepped into Garage 22. With the little light available, I searched for signs of the Bentley, tyre marks. After a few minutes I was able to make out two dark patches deep in the garage, where the front wheels would be. I imagined Mrs Privalova's awkward assistant, nervously turning the steering wheel. I heard the shrill shriek of hard rubber. Two shadows on a slightly lighter background. The residents really existed.

80

"It's Friday."

Harry doesn't turn around.

I'm standing at the door with sleep in my eyes. I button my collar and pull up my tie. It's Friday, I repeat to myself. For some reason, I have to smile. It's Friday. I feel my smile growing wider, my mouth opens. Friday! There is something irresistibly funny about the word. My lips are tight over my gums. I am only just able to control myself. I mustn't think about it. I think of Monday, but that doesn't really help, the distraction is too blatant. I think Monday and hear Friday. I know it's insane to laugh about the name of a day. I try to reduce the pressure in my head by coughing and clearing my throat, by concentrating on my cap, which I arrange at the correct angle. I realize that I have always announced the right day, for so long now, whereas Harry couldn't give a rat's arse what day it is. I could have announced Thursday again today, or Tuesday, he probably wouldn't have noticed. Never having played it on him doesn't make the joke any less funny. I feel my stomach muscles, tense from restrained laughter. It's as if I've been greeting him for weeks now with the announcement that it's Friday and he still hasn't cottoned on. I mustn't laugh out loud, I'd never be able to explain it, he wouldn't believe me. He'll think I'm laughing at him behind his back, because I feel that if I lose it now, I'll crack up completely. As an explanation, Friday will not suffice.

I concentrate on the crown of his head: a flaky, off-white, coin-sized bald spot. His crown is not funny. It's over. I have everything under control again. It's over, I tell myself. Friday. It was funny, terribly funny, but now it's already a lot less funny. Soon it will be over completely.

81

I sit down and ask casually how the night went. At the same time I see that his cap is missing; his relaxed, empty hands are lying on his lap. Where is his cap? Above his beard his cheeks are glowing. He's sweating slightly, his forehead is gleaming, he's staring straight ahead. He seems calm, but it's like he's still recovering from some exertion.

He says, "I caught a fly."

"A fly? You caught a fly?" I hear my words, loud and clear. "That's impossible. You can't have."

Slowly he turns his head towards me.

"The fly must be long dead by now. It's months since I saw it. It's winter."

Harry is dumbstruck.

"It must have laid eggs . . ."

"Eggs? What are you talking about?"

"It can't be the same fly, can it? Did you see the fly? A couple

104

of days after the strawberry jam? I saw a fly then. It was sitting there on the jam stain. Did you see that fly then?"

"No."

"Or hear it? You could hear it really well too."

"What difference does it make, Michel?"

"I'm just curious. It seems so unlikely."

Harry and I gaze into space again. The emptiness is not as empty as I thought. Could the fly have survived on our measly breadcrumbs? How long does a fly live, an ordinary housefly? It must have lain low, saving energy. This basement has laws no-one can escape.

"It wasn't easy," Harry says.

Maybe he coincidentally woke the fly up out of some kind of hibernation.

"I followed it all night, losing sight of it more than once, but I always found it again. Fortunately it was fairly slow. It wasn't really flying, just hovering. But whenever I got close, it shot off with a series of sharp, angular movements and I completely lost track of it. Then suddenly it would be hanging there as cool as you please in front of my nose again. As if it was making fun of me."

It's the same fly or a fly from the same family. Didn't the other eggs mature properly? Is it possible for a fly to have just one descendant?

"A fly," he says, "can't keep flying forever. Eventually it has to land somewhere. I was more patient than the fly. It was an excellent test of my perseverance. Concentrating the whole time and waiting. When it landed on the floor I stalked it. Millimetre by millimetre. So slowly that I might have been able to grab it between my thumb and index finger. I just put my cap down on top of it. I didn't even drop it; I just laid it gently on the floor. It didn't notice a thing."

"Is it still alive?"

"It's under my cap. Between Garages 38 and 39."

Harry stretches his neck and gives the curly hairs a good scratch.

"Can you remember your last shot, Michel? Do you remember when and where you last felt the recoil of your Flock in your wrist?"

I think of the bad guys in the training yard. Funny characters, short and stocky, some of them wearing large flat caps. The mothers with babies in their arms. I hear the quick, high song of the springs pulling on the iron weights, the dry hinges, the clang.

"Wasn't that bliss?" Harry pulls his pistol out of its holster and turns it around dreamily in his hands, looking at it from all sides. "Isn't it a magnificent thing? Look at it." He lays the grip on the palm of his hand then wraps his fingers around it and extends his arm.

For a few seconds the Flock doesn't move.

You could hear a pin drop.

"My last shot of significance," Harry whispers, "was a steel bolt between the eyes of a stupid cow. 'Bang!'" His arm swings up. He looks at me with a melancholy sneer. "Hardly a challenge . . . Shooting a fly out of the air would be a harder task. A test of our ability, you could say. With a bit of luck anyone could hit a stray dog or a bird. But a fly? Wouldn't it be fantastic practice? We slide my cap over to a section with better light. Then we kneel down with our pistols at the ready, lift the cap slowly and wait until the fly has calmed down and takes off again to hover in the air. One shot each. You first."

What happens to a fly that gets struck by a bullet in mid-air? A bullet that, in terms of size, is more or less of the same order of magnitude as the fly? The impact of a direct hit must be similar to that of a fly crashing into a wall with the speed of a bullet.

Since being detached here, we haven't fired a single shot. Harry's always been proud of that; it's proof of our value as the ultimate deterrent, our cold-bloodedness. The organization will be sure to appreciate a remarkable achievement like that and it could very well be the deciding factor that leads to us being promoted.

Unauthorized use of ammunition is an offence of the first degree.

I rub my hands up and down over my face, tracing circles in my forehead with my fingertips. Then I tell him we can't do it. I tell him we can't shoot at the fly.

"Of course not," Harry says, smiling. "You crazy? We're not going to waste bullets on a fly."

He struggles up onto his feet, his night has been long and intense. He collects the case with the brass rods and cleaning cloths.

What would have happened if I'd agreed'

Who would have heard anything?

We have 2,250 cartridges in stock, plus two times fifteen. Winchester, 9mm Luger (Parabellum). The cardboard of the boxes has grown velvety and slack from constant handling and opening. Soon the bottoms will tear off or give way, leaving the cartridges standing on the shelf in protest at their lack of employment, while I hold a tattered scrap of paper in my hand.

"But wouldn't it be fantastic," Harry says. "To take aim, pull the trigger and hit a fly?"

"Yes," I say. "That would be a real experience."

"Imagine the bang. In here!"

"We'd be deaf for a while . . ."

"Cover me."

Harry opens the case and clicks in the safety catch of his Flock 28. I keep my arms stretched out in the direction of the entrance gate, finger on the trigger. In a flash the fifteen cartridges are in the pocket of Harry's jacket and the stripped pistol is spread out on a cloth on his lap. Slide, barrel with chamber, recoil spring guide. The magazine tube, the feeder.

"What do we do with the fly?"

"Kill it," says Harry.

82

Harry and I shake hands, exchange cursory New Year's greetings and fall silent again.

We're sitting at the entrance gate with a tin of corned beef each. We've saved up the last three days' meat ration. It's a moment we've keenly anticipated.

I stand up and listen at the crack. I listen for a minute, two. After about five minutes, my left leg starts to quiver. Just like last year, I can't hear any fireworks going off, neither close by nor in the distance. I don't hear any singing or cheering. I don't hear any guns being fired in celebration. I don't hear anything.

A quarter of an hour later I sit down on the stool. We stay silent, listening attentively to the world beyond the basement. Harry scoops up the meat with the teaspoon. I've cut mine into cubes.

At one o'clock, I stand up again. You never know.

At ten past one, Harry asks if I'm absolutely certain.

I don't answer. I can't be any clearer than that. He always

ignores my date-keeping. Except for New Year's Eve, or rather, New Year's Day, a good hour after midnight.

Harry can go to sleep now but stays sitting.

He says we mustn't fixate on the fireworks, they're meaningless. It's quite possible that the city is still partly populated. Fireworks have been banned for ages and they're very hard to come by . . .

I lean my head back on the entrance gate.

The New Year starts with its slowest minutes.

Shortly after two Harry says that the front, if ever there was such a thing, must be quite far from the city by now. Anyone who stayed and survived would be in hiding.

After another ten minutes of despondent silence, Harry says that we can assume that the situation outside has changed. That the situation must have stabilized. That the unrest, the menace, may have passed . . . I feel his gaze on my face. Do I understand what he's getting at?

I understand what he's getting at.

I ask, "You think so?"

He nods. "I think so. Yes."

I want to make him say it. He brought it up himself. I want us both to hear it from his mouth. I say, "We *are* talking about the same thing, aren't we?"

"The guard," Harry says.

"The guard."

"We have to take it into account, Michel. The plan for a third guard might have been dropped a while ago . . . The organization is an efficient company, they'd never station a superfluous guard somewhere, even if they've announced it. And they don't make those kind of announcements without a reason, I can assure you of that. But that reason can grow less compelling.

109

That's possible . . . They have to constantly assess things and weigh them up. Just like the best guards do too."

He takes off his cap and holds it two-handed in front of his stomach as if it's a book. He gazes into the cap for a while, staring at the dark-blue satin.

"Of course it doesn't mean there's no danger at all."

Harry stands up, pulls his cap down over the top of his head, picks up his empty tin and holds out a hand for mine. "That's why," he says, "the organization decided not to inform us about the cancellation. Subconsciously that could give an illusion of the danger having passed. Which isn't the case."

I watch as Harry marches off to the crusher and disappears around the corner of Garage 34, accompanying him in my thoughts. Along with the new evaluation of our situation, which feels like a change in itself, there's something soothing about the simple fact that his moving has ended our hours of keeping vigil at the entrance. The shrill bang of the tins flashes in two sensitive teeth on my lower right, but the sound I always associate with starving to death is less frightening this time. I hope that Harry will soon whistle, rub his stomach and tell me that no-one can take that away from us now.

"Don't forget, Michel," he starts in the distance, "that cancelling the guard does not reflect on our qualities at all. It doesn't change our record of service either, so it can't affect our prospects of making the elite."

He's right. We haven't discredited ourselves in any way.

"What we need," Harry says, after rejoining me at the gate, standing there with one hand on the back of the chair and the other on his hip. "What we need . . ."

"Is an opportunity," I say, continuing for him, "to distinguish ourselves from our fellow guards."

110

"No, Michel. Yes, of course, but the point is," Harry says, abruptly shifting his attention to the emergency lighting on the ceiling, "we can no longer wait for that opportunity to present itself." He moves directly under a light and looks up. "It's up to us to think of a way to prove ourselves and draw attention to ourselves. We have to speed up our promotion ourselves."

He fetches the chair and puts it under the light fitting. He asks me for the stool and positions it on the seat of the chair. Carefully he ascends the unstable construction.

Using both hands, he investigates the cover over the emergency light. Going by the movement of his right wrist, he seems to be using his thumbnail, which is definitely long enough, to unscrew a screw. Three screws later he passes the lukewarm cover down to me. The smell wafting up out of it is old and stale, the flies have dried to dust. He removes his jacket and takes the precaution of using the sleeve to grip the tube. He is patient. He turns, pushes and levers. Until finally the light goes off.

83

We work towards our room, extinguishing fourteen of the sixteen lights. Harry suggests leaving the covers on the floor; we never walk through the middle of the basement anyway. We arrange the covers perpendicular to the route from the entrance to the lifts, spreading them out at the same time to increase the chance of an intruder kicking one.

Seen from the bunkroom door, the light from the remaining two tubes falls to the floor like a curtain, making everything behind it invisible so that we, on the chair and the stool, feel like we are on display in a shop window. In theory and with a lot of luck, an intruder could approach unnoticed to within twenty metres.

After a few minutes, Harry says we have to do this properly. We either do it properly or not at all. No half measures. We both know the floor plan by heart. He says that in time, when we're used to it, we will be able to see more in complete darkness than now, and definitely much more than someone coming into the basement from the light outside. They'd be as blind as a bat. He swears in surprise, too excited to stay sitting. "That's it," he says. "That's it, Michel. We'll show the organization that we don't need any night goggles, not you and me, we can keep guard in complete darkness without them." He starts laughing. He can't believe it. Why didn't we think of this ages ago? He laughs so hard he bares his yellowed teeth, then thumps me on the shoulder and wishes me a Happy New Year a second time.

84

When I'm relaxing on the stool, the darkness is a casing that fits me perfectly, my personal cocoon. When I'm doing a round, the darkness is almost tangible, an object with a beginning and an end, something you can bump into. The first days are awkward, but we get through them thanks to the habits we have maintained for such a long time. My having counted my footsteps on patrol is especially convenient. All day long Harry and I direct short sentences at each other. The way of answering, the sound

112

and volume allow us to precisely determine the other's location and state of mind. Two submarines in the depths of the ocean, using sonar to gauge the other's presence.

They are exciting days. Time passes more slowly, but the days are fuller and seem more purposeful. We experience more in the dark. Liberated from the dominance of sight, the other senses achieve their full potential. We can't escape them, they demand our attention and bring out sides of the basement we have scarcely noticed before. By disappearing, the basement has become more emphatically present.

We no longer click on the lights in the bunkroom, toilet and storeroom either. They blind us. The time it takes to readjust to the darkness in the rest of the basement could one day prove fatal. The light in our lives is limited to the lights in our watches; that's enough to keep the calendar up to date. We're careful with them and never look straight at the lit dial. In case of danger, we have agreed to flash three times.

The bright rod of daylight protruding at an angle through the crack next to the entrance gate remains hidden behind Garage 1. Although it doesn't disturb our darkness, I tear a strip off my sheet and twist the material to make a plug for the opening.

85

Winged horses, white, a whole flock of them, a white cloud, landing one after the other, falling out of the sky like clumsy starlings and stumbling over their forelegs. Their long heads whip down on their long necks and dash against the ground. I feel my face twist. A short circuit in their brains, a genetic imperfection; horses should stay on the ground. I blink once, ten times, it makes no difference. I remain concentrated. I am awake and on guard duty. I am inside the body that squats, sits, stands or walks; what difference does it make in the dark? Eighteen times seven. A hundred and forty minus fourteen. One hundred and twenty-six. I am picking pears. My hand appears and grabs. I feel the snap as the tree releases the stem. We are under strict supervision. I push my long nails through the rough peel and into the flesh. Voluptuously, I suck my fingers. One image supplants the other. I can't stop them. They slip by or change abruptly. My leg. I pull my leg up, suction, the rubber boot is stuck in the mud. The bandage on my foot is brown, the bleeding staunched, but the pain . . . In the shade of a tree I am wearing a bowler hat, an insignificant little man asks where my boot has got to. I point at the magnolia, alone in the grassy field. The velvet buds have already burst open. Coconuts, the roar of the surf and a child, a girl, hardly four, struggling through the sand. She pushes her tummy out in front of her, and looks up with one glaring blue eye, poking me in the thigh with a finger. She says something, but it's lost. I drop to my knees, she hugs me as if it's a farewell, a reunion, sorrow or joy; it doesn't matter. Her voice tickles in my ear. "Is it already morning?" Her question cleaves a hairy coconut, the white, the juice, as fresh as pure love. I want to preserve her in formaldehyde, I'll keep her in a jar, arranging her pink virgin lips in a smile. I fill in a label and stick it on near the bottom. Coming ready or not.

86

I am calmer than ever. I didn't jump when I heard the colossal mechanism start up. Nobody appears in the night-time light streaming in through the half-open entrance gate. It is not night-time light, it is more a shadow, free of artificial lighting or moonlight, a slightly different version of darkness over there, past Garage 1, on the far side of the basement; I can point it out. The gate can't be any higher than a metre above ground level. I am sitting motionless outside the bunkroom door. Yes, I am almost sure of that. I'm calm. It's a nightmare threatening to take shape before my eyes, but I've always been prepared for the worst. I know what's coming and what I have to do. I am a guard. I won't need to think. My self-assurance surprises me and I wonder how long it will last. I have to keep thinking, especially when I feel it's no longer necessary. A scream germinates in the back of my mind. This is no optical and aural illusion because the gate starts up again: the shadow disappears, the shock of the heavy gate on the concrete. I feel it all the way over here – in my feet, up through the legs of the stool and in my bottom – I'm as sensitive as an insect's antennae. Then a flash, a pinprick deep in my brain. I grab the Flock, smothering the scream and blinking away tears. I hear cautious footsteps, still a hundred metres away, coming closer. Where else could they go? In the blinking, an explosion of spots and patches on the inside of my eyelids; in the basement, a torch being waved around, unable to reveal me at this distance, even if it's pointed in my direction. Which it hardly ever is: it shines on the garages and their numbers, always indicated by large digits on the left, and on the emergency lighting covers, seals spread out over a dark beach. Walnut. Unmistakable. Harry is awake and has crept out of the bunk-room, taking up position on the chair without the slightest sound. The smell is strong; he's in his vest. I don't dare to turn my head out of fear the movement will betray us. I stay in my cocoon. For now, I hold the hand with the Flock low. We have to wait. Will Harry give me a sign? Our nerves will be put to the test. The closer we allow the intruder to approach, the greater our chance of eliminating him with a single shot each. But the chance of one of us being hit increases as well. It's clear that he is in unknown territory; he hasn't grasped the layout of the basement yet. Or is he looking for a particular garage in which something of great value is stored? In that case we can simply enclose him and shoot him dead. The torch is now sweeping the floor, moving back and forth in wider and wider arcs as if he's sowing light. I can't make out even a glimpse of the intruder himself. He has reached the middle of the basement. I judge it the moment to aim my Flock, gradually, with the intruder still at a distance, adjusting my position. Right away my extended arms begin to tremble under their own weight, but not from fatigue: I will be able to maintain this pose for a long time, as long as it takes. Betting on him being right-handed, I aim to the right of the light and a little higher, at the breast. He is walking straight into our trap, we don't have to do a thing. Then he stops and shines the torch down in front of his feet, holding it still. The arc of light extends to within a couple of metres of the toes of our shoes. He has obviously noticed something. My index finger has almost squeezed the trigger. "Hello? Are you there?" A deep bass, suggesting a big man. Harry remains silent and so do I. One more step towards us and he's dead. But the man stays where he is. "Are you there?" Above the light I've seen a flash of white: teeth. I aim the Flock a fraction higher. "It's me," he says. "The guard."

TWO

TWO

87

"Who sent you?"

The guard keeps the torch aimed at his feet, presumably over-whelmed by Harry's bellow, which echoes off the walls, harassing him from all sides.

"Who's your employer?"

"The organization," we hear, deep and calm.

"We've got our guns on you. Put the torch on the floor, light down. Then take three steps back."

I see the beam of light contract and concentrate as a blinding disc, which is swallowed by the concrete.

"Where are your colleagues?"

"My colleagues?"

"The other two guards. Your comrades."

"I don't know. I'm alone."

"You're alone?"

"Yes."

"Without any colleagues?"

After a moment's consideration, "You're my colleagues."

Harry falls silent. He doesn't stand up. I hear a deep dragging sound as he sucks breath into his lungs. The disillusionment has hit him hard. I decide to take the lead, ordering the guard further back. I count his steps. At five I tell him to stop. As I walk towards the torch, Harry moves off to one side to cover me and make sure he doesn't shoot me in the back by accident.

Shining the light on the guard, I immediately see the familiar uniform, the crease in the trousers, the emblem: he's one of us. Remarkably, the uniform seems to be standing up by itself, enclosing a figure that's gigantic but absent. Then I see the whites of eyes under his cap, flicking on and off like two small beacons. I have to use my imagination in combination with the matt gleam of his pitch-black skin to make out his head against the darkness of the basement.

Under his arm he is holding a large cardboard box, whose bottom is bulging from the weight of its contents. He's carrying it effortlessly, casually, as if it's a beach ball that would blow away if he let go of it.

88

The torch is standing the other way round on the ground and casting a glow on the ceiling, so that it feels like we're sheltering from the darkness under a tarpaulin of light. I don't know what I'm eating. I recognize the taste: it's fruit, in syrup, I must have eaten it before. I can't put a name to it and at the moment I couldn't care less. My left hand squeezes the enormous tin, at least five times the size of a corned beef tin and all mine. I concentrate on eating, greedily gulping down pieces of soft slippery fruit, chewing just long enough to avoid choking. Peach. I'm dizzy with excitement and haste. Harry's eating frankfurters, stuffing them into his cheeks and washing them down with the liquid they came in. We're eating as if the cardboard box isn't filled to the top with tins. Extraordinary colours and shapes we haven't seen for years, but they leave the guard cold. He doesn't say a word, watching us indifferently. He's sitting on his backside on the ground on the other side of the box and the torch. Kneeling and full of mistrust, we keep our eyes on him as if he could take the food away from us again at any moment.

89

Harry grabs the torch and shines it in the guard's face from close by. The whites of his eyes are yellowish, but not unhealthy. The irises are so dark they're absent. The pupils, provocatively large as a result, seem to go against the laws of nature by dilating in the bright light.

In answer to Harry's question as to what's going on outside, the guard shrugs. He claims to have spent an hour or two sitting in the back of a vehicle before they dropped him off. He couldn't see anything and he didn't hear anything either. He asks sheepishly if we can tell him what our location is. No, he doesn't know, he was picked up without any explanation and brought here. At his previous post he was prohibited from communicating with his colleague, who manned the next box a little further down the road. He doesn't know why: he was used to it, he was taught not to ask questions. It was a remote storage depot. He's not able, or allowed, to tell us any more. No, he has no idea, but whatever it was, the capacity must have been enormous. Besides his colleague, the guard never saw anyone in the complex. There could have been fifty guards stationed there, it might have been just the two of them. He speaks calmly, his words babble along; that's just the way things go.

His stubble is extremely unusual, in my eyes at least, a white man's eyes. The hairs are stuck together in little knobs that look stiff and hard. On his cheeks they're spread out with lots of space between them, lonely, as if they don't actually belong there. On his chin they're closer together, but not close enough to cover the skin.

90

Harry stays aloof. For the first few hours he's too unsteady from the blow to pay much attention to the guard. He answers my suggestion of temporarily turning three of the lights back on with silent assent. After all, the guard needs an opportunity to familiarize himself with the peculiarities of the location as quickly as possible.

While the guard and I set to work with the chair, the stool and the light covers – with Harry in position near the entrance gate – I think about the specific smell I noticed after eating the tinned fruit, when the tension had become a little more bearable. We're reconnecting the lights along the longitudinal axis of the basement, which we have divided neatly into equal segments. That is still very far from lighting all of the corners. We give the guard a floor plan too and let him keep his torch, which is now swinging from a loop that is attached to the waistband of his trousers, but missing from ours. I decide that the smell of his body tends towards the odour of scorched horse's hooves, albeit strongly diluted.

91

Harry grits his teeth and looks down at the toes of his shoes, his clenched jaw muscles distorting his face. The guard takes a discreet step backwards. He'll have to lie down somewhere, but there are only two beds, even if both of them are free when the guard is allowed to sleep his hours, because from now on a minimum of two guards will patrol together at all times.

I've come up with a rotation system for the chair and the stool. Every two hours we move over so that someone else has to either sit on the ground or stay standing. This only applies in the daytime, during the hours we're all awake, and doesn't include the time we spend on patrol.

We were going to apply a similar system to the flannels and towels, which I wash weekly, but in the end Harry couldn't reconcile himself to the prospect. A few minutes later he made a gruff offer to donate his pillowcase, from which we could tear a washcloth and a cloth for the guard to dry himself.

The guard said that was a fine suggestion and thanked Harry for his generosity. It didn't sound like an ambiguous remark to me, but I might have been mistaken. The guard always speaks in the same deep tone, at the same tempo. It's difficult to tell how he really means things. His face stays the same. It's coarsely modelled, like the rest of his body: in combination with the uniform, it evokes memories of old footage of military dictators in sweltering African countries.

92

"Has Harry told you something about the building?"

"No," the guard says. "Harry hasn't done that."

We've only just started the inspection round and I feel obliged to talk. We are alone in each other's company for the first time. I find it hard to believe that Harry didn't speak a word to the guard in the five hours I was asleep. Maybe it's a matter of persevering. Maybe not talking starts to feel natural after fifteen minutes of silence, making continuing in the same vein simpler for both parties and a more pleasant alternative.

I guide the guard while walking next to him, my purposeful footsteps making it clear that we don't neglect a single corner of the basement. It's like a dance he hasn't yet mastered, partly because his paces are longer than mine, less manoeuvrable. As far as the inspection round is concerned, I'm a better instructor than Harry. Now and then, in the darkest sections, the guard clicks on his torch because he's lost track of me.

On the way back to the lifts, I say, "It's better not to talk in the vicinity of the entrance gate."

"Yes, I understand that."

"It's a forty-storey building."

"Forty," he says. "Forty storeys."

It sounds like he's questioning the figure. Has someone told him different? Or had he expected more than forty?

"There's a lobby on the ground floor, but that's just for show.

There's no entrance there. This is the entrance."

We stop in front of the three lifts: something from the distant past, a strange historical phenomenon we've come to briefly view.

"Residents, staff, visitors."

He's not particularly impressed and doesn't ask me to elaborate. He seems to me like a man who is seldom impressed or upset. He lives inside his body, his fortress. Wherever that body might be, whatever the company or situation, it's irrelevant. He is always safe at home.

Although, in essence, his arrival is bad news for us, there is also a good side. We are now in greater numbers to resist hostilities. More than anything, I feel a degree of excitement. Whatever else, the organization hasn't forgotten us. The guard is living proof that they have been appreciating us in silence the whole time.

We continue our patrol: past the bunkroom door, which is open so that the sleeping guard will be woken by the first hint of an engagement. Inside the light is turned off. A few metres further along I lay my hand flat against the toilet door without pushing it open. "There is something I have to tell you," I tell the guard. "Something about the toilet. More specifically, something about flushing the toilet. It's important that you listen carefully."

93

The guard has withdrawn to the bunkroom for his night's sleep when Harry gives me an angry little poke near Garage 12. "Couldn't you have objected?"

"Objected?"

"Yes, objected. You just stood there like a sheep. You could have rejected the suggestion out of hand. Didn't it even occur to you to object?"

Apparently Harry's grievances are not insurmountable because he keeps walking.

"And why were you so keen to start ripping it? It looked like you were enjoying it. What were you thinking? I'll lend the poor twerp a helping hand?"

"Harry, it was your own suggestion."

"We have more right to a pillowcase than somebody who's just strolled in here. Am I wrong? How long have we been here now? Hey, Michel? You and me, how long? Tell me. If you ask me, long enough to have a right to a pillowcase. My own pillowcase. That's what I think about it."

"The linen isn't ours," I offer later. "It's property of the organization, we can't lay any claim to it."

"Then you should have objected to the destruction of organization kit. We've committed an offence. Fourth degree."

"If you like, you can use mine."

"Of course not. Keep your pillowcase."

The realization that the guard is now sleeping in my bed, between my sheets, with his head on my pillow must have finally got through to Harry. Things could be worse, much worse.

"Why didn't you tell him anything about the building?"

"Did he say that?"

"I asked him. I asked if you'd already told him something about the building. He said no."

"Did he ask you anything?"

"No."

"Me neither. Not a thing. Nada. Did you tell him anything?"

"A few things. General stuff. Why didn't you?"

"He kept his mouth shut. He didn't give a peep so I thought, then I'll keep my mouth shut too. I don't want him thinking I'm going to bend over backwards and get all chatty just 'cause he's come to reinforce us."

"He's new."

"Doesn't matter. Or maybe it does. You started talking first, remember? When you came."

The memory brings a smile to his face.

"There was just the two of us. This is different."

With revived interest, I pull the plug out of the crack to the side of the entrance gate. I peer first with my left eye, then with my right. The view hasn't changed. The bare tree against the night sky, which is clear. Yes, clear. Have I ever seen it like this, so very clear? There is no wind. I can't make out many stars, but the sky is still clear. I can tell from the tree and its branches, which are black with sharp edges and not hazy at all. No shadows cast by a full moon outside my field of vision. Is it because I haven't looked for so long? I stick my nose into the opening. Stone and iron, the familiar smell. With a touch of rot in the mix. Wet, dead leaves.

"There's no comparison," I whisper. "When I arrived you were here alone and the residents were still living in the building. It's totally different for the guard."

"Did he say anything about it?"

"About what?"

"The residents. Their not being here, with one exception."

"No."

"Did you say anything about it?"

"I don't think so."

"You don't think so?"

"I'm sure of it."

"Don't you find that a little strange? He doesn't even ask what's going on. We're totally used to it, but it must be very weird for him, not seeing any residents, not a single car in the car park. Think about it, Michel. Wouldn't you find it strange? I know I would."

Deep in thought we pace the invisible line of our inspection route. At the bunkroom door we hear light snoring. His sleep, too, seems untroubled.

94

In the daytime there are moments I forget him for minutes at a time. Generally when it's his turn to stand: Harry on the chair and me on the stool. He never sits on the ground, none of us do. I forget him. Then I see him again as if in a vision. He's as large as life but not really here; I'm imagining him. Harry and I are on guard duty in the basement alone. Soon we'll hear the service lift. It's Claudia. She's bringing us a plate covered with an upturned soup bowl. Lamb stew. A black giant. With kidneys, eyes and a backbone. It's too drastic to accept as reality. And yet he's standing here, leaning against the wall with a loaded Flock 28 on his hip. Breathing the same air as us.

When Harry and I talk to each other it's like we're putting on a play. Our words fall into their fixed patterns, the sentences are old friends, but the dialogue sounds stilted and rehearsed. The presence of an observer in the darkness behind the footlights changes us into a couple of hams. The guard himself doesn't say much and hardly a word in Harry's presence. He does display an occasional tendency to briefly repeat statements or phrases, including some that are totally trivial, for no apparent reason. Is he taking mental notes that inadvertently leak out of his mouth? Do they combine to form a report he leafs through once more just before falling asleep?

95

After a single five-hour night the linen is saturated with his body odour, which mine is powerless to resist. It is not as pungent as Harry's, not as sharp, but strong all the same. According to Harry there can be no doubt about it: the last resident is in acute danger. That's why they've sent the guard after all. The danger is evidently so acute that the organization didn't have time to arrange things properly and is counting on us being able to share the linen peacefully in the meantime. He doesn't exclude the possibility of a logistic follow-up. Maybe within a couple of days. A week at most.

I hear their footsteps build up and then fade back into silence and each time I hope it's the last time I've heard it, that I'm about to fall asleep. I've got three hours left, I have to relax. The pistol is lying on my stomach with the barrel pointing at the door. I practise what I hope will be a controlled reflex.

After yet another pass, I slip out of bed. Barefoot, I look out through the opening into the basement proper, lit by three fading fluorescent tubes. Harry and the guard don't deviate from the set trajectory. I can hardly make them out. I don't think they're talking. Sometimes I see the movement of feet and legs, but rarely higher than the knees. They seem to be avoiding the light, circumnavigating it as if strolling on the banks of a deep pond. Still black water that makes you gasp for breath. If you go under, you'll never resurface.

96

The guard says he spoke to him twice. I jump and realize I was almost nodding off; I only got an hour's broken sleep. I can't remember asking any questions. Not Harry – his previous colleague, the one in the next box. He went to see him twice, even though it wasn't allowed. Speaking to colleagues was forbidden. He has no idea why, but it wasn't his favourite rule and in the end he broke it twice. He wants to know if that bothers me. I shrug. He asks me to be honest. I tell him it's nothing to do with me and water under the bridge anyway. It's in the past, he doesn't have to worry about it anymore. He shakes his head disparagingly, straightens his shoulders and takes a deep breath: he shouldn't have done it. It's something he will never be able to undo. Rules are rules and a guard has to respect them. He understands my disapproval and also my reluctance to express it bluntly. He says he's deeply sorry about it. It was stronger than he was. One day he saw his colleague waving. The gesture was unmistakable. It was a greeting, directed at him. He waved back; as far as he knew greetings were not forbidden. It started very innocently, with a full sixty metres separating them. While the guard blathers on, I wonder what's got into him: he's talking as if we've already spent two days walking around chatting together. I don't think I've asked him anything. He says that they were best friends long before they exchanged a word with each other. He can't explain it, but it was something he just knew, he knew it for a fact. He had a sleeping schedule, presumably adjusted for a skeleton security staff, and he followed it precisely. After waking up he always prepared himself quickly and went to stand in front of his box with his heart in his throat. Almost always, his friend waved to him straight away, asking with a thumbs-up sign if everything was O.K. After his friend had gone to bed himself a little later, the guard kept his eye on his watch and made sure to look in the direction of that box about five hours later when it was time for him to reappear. It was like that every day. They were best friends, anyone could see that.

97

Harry grabs my sleeve. With gentle pressure, he pulls me into the narrow gap between Garages 34 and 35. It's pitch black, but

Harry doesn't slow down. At the first crusher I feel his hands grasping my shoulders as he pushes me up against the iron wall. His face is close, his breath as warm as blood.

"Back to the start," he says.

"How do you mean?"

"Where he asks you what you think about it."

"He was talking about rules, the regulations, and him breaching them. He was very sorry about it."

"And he wanted you to be honest? About what you thought of his offence?"

"Yes, he honestly wanted my opinion."

"Did you give it to him?"

"Not really. I just said it was water under the bridge. Then he said he understood it, my disapproval. He understood my not wanting to express it in so many words."

"What was your answer to that?"

"Nothing. He was in the wrong of course."

"I know that. But you didn't add anything else?"

"No."

"Was that the first time he's made a confession or admitted something?"

"It was a complete surprise, Harry. He just launched into the story. I was dumbstruck."

I hear him scratching his throat, his fingernails rasping through the curling hairs. "So they give each other the thumbs-up now and then and wave hello . . ."

"He said they were best friends. He just knew it."

"Best friends?"

"Yes, he was convinced of it. He thought so, anyway."

"He was wrong?"

"I don't know. I don't know what to make of his story. One

day he sees the guard make a gesture he doesn't understand. Not giving him the thumbs-up or waving, but something less obvious, surreptitious, from the hip. After fretting for a couple of hours, he decides that something might be going on; it must have been some kind of signal. He said that a friend in need is a friend indeed. He asked me if he was right. If a friend in need was a friend indeed."

"He asked you that?"

"Yes. He made a point of it. I said I hoped so."

"And what did he say to that?"

"He nodded. He hoped so too. And what happens? That friend of his is rather upset by his visit. He tells the guard to piss off. He knows it's against the rules, doesn't he? But we're friends, says the guard. He says that a friend in need is a friend indeed. His colleague puts a finger to his lips and keeps his mouth shut. Meanwhile the guard has cast a glance into the sentry box: it's identical to his. Different colours, that's all. He sees a simple figurine on a shelf, a porcelain cat. There are others too, five or six, but not on the shelf. Back in his box he can't get that figurine out of his head. When he sees his own bare shelf, he thinks of that white pussycat. It has a blissful smile on its face and its long-lashed eyes are closed, and it's made so you can put it against the wall or next to some object and it will look like it's rubbing up against it."

"Are you taking the piss?"

"That's how he told me about it, in one big gush. There's more. The next day the guard goes back. After having brooded about the incident all night, he throws caution to the wind and goes over to his friend's sentry box a second time. And again, wordlessly, the friend shows him the door. The guard says that although he appreciates his colleague's desire to stick to the rules, he still finds his behaviour extremely unfriendly. As a token of his good character he could lend him the figurine on the shelf. After all, he has figurines to spare, whereas he doesn't have a single one. He'll take good care of it and bring it back at the end of his service. He says that since their last meeting he's had to think about that pussycat constantly, he found it so beautiful. But his colleague snatches the figurine from the shelf and threatens to throw it down on the ground and smash it to smithereens if the guard doesn't get the hell out of there . . ."

Harry doesn't react.

"That's his story," I say.

"That's it?"

"That's it."

"How's it end?"

"I don't know. He clammed up. He didn't say another word. I guess he just slinked off."

98

I get Harry to smell too; reluctantly he puts his nose in the crack. The wind is blowing straight at the gate again and carrying silence, the silence of the country, I think. Maybe the country-side starts just a couple of kilometres away. The smell of rotting leaves is almost gone. Instead I think I can detect manure. At least, it's the smell I associate with manure. A steaming mixture of hay and dung, shovelled out of a shed and spread on a field. Has agriculture recovered? Will the crops grow normally? Will the harvest be any good, will it be edible? Or is the farmer ignoring my questions and doing what he's done his whole life: farming. Hoisting himself up onto the seat of his old tractor and chugging over his fields with his last few litres of fuel. Preparing the soil for sowing regardless of any prohibitions or restrictions that have been put in place, despite the warnings of a poison he can neither see nor smell. Acting instinctively by following his nature, true to the calendar and the seasons. Wearing the threadbare blue overalls that are more familiar to him than his own wife. Carrying on the way a cow produces milk, a chicken lays eggs and a pig just grows. Is that possible, two kilometres from here? A bent-over farmer, chickens scratching in the dirt, a nervous mutt? Cows shoulder to shoulder in a muggy shed? Sparrows chirping in the farmyard. Harry turns away from the gate. As if he can read my thoughts, he purses his lips and shakes his head. He can't smell any manure. Plus, he says, it would be unusual anyway. The tree is bare, not a leaf in sight, not even any buds. It's too early for ploughing and farming. Unless they're piling the dung from the sheds on the fields in preparation. But him, he can't smell a thing.

99

We've just started moving again, in step, when Harry suddenly stops. Half a step ahead of him I prick up my ears, hand on my Flock. The buzzing of the middle tube keeps getting deeper, the end is near. I am trying to concentrate on sounds from the sally port between the street and the entrance gate when Harry says that the guard deliberately left his story unfinished. Because he wants us to keep thinking about it. That's exactly what he wants. He very consciously left it open, without a conclusion. Whereas the outcome of the story and what we think about it are actually irrelevant and meant to distract us from the heart of the matter. That's obvious! It's not about that stupid porcelain figurine. Am I mad? A pussycat to put on his shelf? What a load of bull. Come on. What kind of guard has porcelain figurines in his sentry box? He wants me to tell him that. He asks me if I've ever heard anything so ridiculous, porcelain figurines in a sentry box? When I shake my head, he hisses emphatically, See! He tells me the guard is a sly one. And to think that someone like me, who's been to university – now pointing a finger at my chest – didn't see through his trick at once! The guard deliberately wove an absurd detail into his story – porcelain figurines – to make Harry and me think, This is so extraordinary, it can't be made up. Damn sneaky.

When I ask why it's so important for the guard to have us believe his story, Harry says, Confession. Because that was what it was after all, a confession. It was a confession of a breach of regulations he's fabricated to the best of his abilities. What can that mean?

Harry is going to tell me what it means and as he whispers the words into existence, I realize that his understanding has only just preceded them. Didn't the guard ask me to be honest? Hadn't he understood my disapproval, which I didn't even need to express? Hadn't he been immensely sorry for a violation that was essentially rather trivial? For Harry it's as plain as the nose on my face: the guard's half-baked confession was designed to lure me into his net. He wanted to arouse my sympathies, pretending to open up his heart to me to draw me out, trying to tempt me into confessing violations that were possibly worse than his, committed here in this very basement. That was his goal. That was what he was after. Come on, Harry says. First absolutely nothing, two days with his lips sealed and then suddenly a whole spiel? Do I think that's normal? He wants me to tell him that. He thought all along that the explanation was bizarre: why wouldn't two guards be allowed to speak to each other? Why doesn't he know where he was stationed or what he was guarding? And then out of the blue, up and at it, off he goes, sixty metres to visit his friend for a chat? Get out of here.

100

I stand on tiptoe and press down on the grey mass with my full weight, arms straight. Puddles of grey suds appear around my fists, only to be absorbed again by the sheets the moment I stop pushing. Harry is keeping watch at the entrance gate, the guard is at the bunkroom door, which is wide open; his figure fills the doorway. He looks over his shoulder and asks if it's O.K., if he shouldn't help. He likes getting his hands wet, he doesn't mind it at all. He wants to thank me. For letting him sleep in my bed and being willing to share my sheets with him. That is, he says, a friendly gesture. The least he can do is wash the sheets himself. I'm wary. At the same time I do my best to sound casual when I say that I prefer to do it myself, that I'm used to it. It's no picnic in a small washbasin, there's a knack to it. Before you know it, I hear myself joking, the whole room's flooded. Yes, the guard replies earnestly, he understands. The whole room flooded. He turns back to the basement proper and crosses his arms, his arched shoulders pulling his blue jacket tight.

He is a remarkable figure. As remarkable as the porcelain figurines in his supposed friend's sentry box. Maybe that's a tried and tested tactic the organization uses for its special agents, the guards who, besides guarding something, inspect other guards while they're at it. Maybe the organization always deploys striking characters for that purpose, characters who are so striking it doesn't occur to the guards under surveillance to suspect them of anything, least of all a secret and highly delicate evaluation. It's just too implausible.

Harry and I can fulfil our duties alone, we don't need anyone's help, that's what we need to show the guard. He knows exactly what's going on outside, what we're up against and the dangers we can expect. Harry says he's deliberately keeping us in the dark so that the lack of information and resulting tension will test our mental resilience to the limit. But we're not soft. We won't weep and beg and bombard him with questions. It doesn't bother us, it just hones our concentration. Like always, we work independently. We're attuned to each other and don't need anyone else. Harry is right. We stay calm and just do our job. That's all we need to do, he says. As soon as we start to act strangely, the guard will know we've unmasked him and our evaluation will be compromised. We have to make sure we don't give ourselves away. That's why I'm being wary. I play along blithely, but keep a certain distance. From this point, Harry says, we've as good as made it. The darkness when he arrived must have made quite an impression on the guard. He's seen the primitive conditions we've survived; now he's experiencing them first hand. As long as the situation with the resident doesn't get out of hand, we've got it all wrapped up. In no time Harry and I will be out in the fresh air in the uniform of the elite.

101

The guard runs his gaze over the well-ordered shelves. It's the first time I've taken him into the storeroom with me. I detect a measure of surprise in the dark gleam of his eyes, bordering on childish joy at the precision with which the boxes are arranged. Are other guards less meticulous? Or is it recognition of a case of best practice?

"Don't touch!"

Startled, he pulls his hand back as if he's burnt his fingertips on a red-hot box.

"I mean the cardboard's got fairly soft. They could rip."

"Rip?" His voice is flat.

"Yes, rip. I carry out an inspection every day, so I know how to pick them up. Someone who's not used to it would tear one of those boxes straight away."

I realize that I've used the word "inspection".

The guard moves closer to the shelves and stares at the Winchester cowboy, before reading the details on the label out loud. It's as if he's making another of his mental notes despite having exactly the same cartridges in the pistol on his hip.

"Shall I show you?"

He nods vaguely, but looks at the top row with interest. I slide out a box, demonstrating how I squeeze the cartridges together at the bottom, between thumb and index finger, so that the cardboard doesn't have to carry any of the weight. The pressure has to be just right. A touch too little and the cartridges could suddenly fall through the bottom, a touch too much and there's a chance of them pushing past each other, hopelessly breaking out of their rectangle and irreparably crumpling the weakened box.

The guard understands and immediately masters the technique. He is elated by his success. "Now we can both do it," he says.

He lays a hand on my shoulder, a bear's paw, briefly tightening around the top of my arm.

I feel a strange smile on my face.

"But, of course, you'd rather I left them alone," the guard says, carefully sliding the box back into the row. "I understand. You being used to it."

I can't come up with anything better than a slight shrug; a mild protest seems the least risky at this stage. I reach up past his face to get the first box down from the top shelf, open it and count the cartridges.

102

Harry says he heard us. He heard me and the guard talking to each other. It sounds like a casual remark that requires neither confirmation nor explanation, but several minutes later, far from the bunkroom door, he adds that he slept terribly. I ask him if those two things are related, which is something I can hardly imagine: the guard and I were always careful to keep our voices down near the room. Harry must have been wide awake to even tell our voices apart from so far into the basement. He doesn't answer. He asks what the guard said. I need to think about it for a couple of steps; the five endless hours have blurred together. I can't remember very much, an exchange of generalities about the profession. Harry wants to know if he made any more confessions. Nothing about porcelain figurines or suchlike? he asks contemptuously. He turns his head and gives me a meaningful look. No, I say, nothing like that. After a few minutes' silence, Harry says again that he clearly heard us talking. I don't understand what he's getting at. It's as if I've claimed the contrary. I tell him I'm sorry if our voices kept him awake, but would nonetheless be surprised if they had. He takes a while to react and that makes his reaction, if possible, even more astonishing. He asks if the guard is funny. Funny? Yes, funny. He heard me laughing. Maybe, Harry says, the guard has a side he only shows me. A funny side, because he clearly heard me laughing. The words rasp out of his throat, bitter on his tongue, as if we have shamelessly kept him awake. No, I say. If I laughed, it wasn't because of any jokes. The guard is no humorist.

103

Harry is sitting on the chair, left of the bunkroom door. The guard is on the stool to the right. I stand behind him and slowly tip his head back until his skull is resting against my stomach or, more accurately, my chest; he's a good bit bigger than Harry. The paring knife is blunt. There are notches on the blade that tug painfully on the hairs. But the stiff knobs on his cheek have short, compact stems that are much easier to cut than our separate beard hairs. I only need to move the blade slightly to feel numerous hairs in the bundle give way. The hair is also coarser than ours so that the knife seems to grip better.

It still takes me a good hour to pick the harvest on the guard's face. All that time Harry stares sternly into the middle of the basement. Now and then a sigh escapes his distended nostrils. The frizzy hair on the guard's head is too intimidating. It's like there's a cap over the top of it holding it together. I wouldn't know where to start.

The guard goes into the bunkroom to wash his face and – after giving himself an extended appraisal in the mirror – returns with a beaming smile. He pulls his tie tighter, rubs his cheeks and thanks me. He says I've done a good job. He's as happy as if he's received an unexpected, beautiful gift. He says he looks good. And a lot younger too, I add. Harry jumps up, the legs of the chair scraping back over the floor. He hesitates for a moment, as if surprised by his own action, then resolutely reaches for his Flock. In no time the guard and I are pointing our cocked pistols at the entrance too. The guard stays at his post; Harry and I creep closer along opposite sides of the open space, metre by metre. Nothing unusual at the gate. We keep watch without speaking or moving. Outside it's deathly silent. The building could be on the moon. After half an hour Harry shakes his head. We look at each other in the darkness, still listening. Then Harry shakes his head again and holsters his pistol. False alarm.

104

Harry pulls me into the bunkroom by the arm, whispering that I have to come and have a look, quick. The guard has just got up. He has dressed and withdrawn to the toilet and that can take quite a while. The narrow sleeping area is saturated with his smell and warmer than the rest of the basement. At the wash-basin Harry steps to one side so I can come up next to him. Shoulder to shoulder we stand before the mirror, but Harry directs his gaze lower. He tells me to have a good look. Hanging over the edge of the grey washbasin are two identical flannels and a piece of pillowcase. Harry asks if I'm blind or what. I look closely. My flannel on the left, Harry's flannel on the right, the guard's washrag in the middle. Harry claims it's not the first time. I stare and wrack my brains until suddenly Harry grabs my hand, pushes it down on his flannel for a couple of seconds and then on the guard's washrag. One is cold and wet, the other dry. He says, somewhat superfluously, that he washed himself five hours ago and always wrings out the flannel. The guard just washed and his rag is as dry as a bone. Still holding my hand, Harry asks if he needs to draw me a picture. We look at each other in the mirror. His eyes are sunken but wide open. He asks if I under-stand what's going on here.

105

It's not the first time. I have to realize that. Maybe it's the kind
of thing I would never have expected from the guard, Harry says
with a touch of triumph in his voice. Him trying to stir things up
like this. And isn't it peculiar, to say the least, that the guard
doesn't ever speak to Harry? He wants me to explain that to him.
When he's the one who donated his pillowcase to him. What, do
I think, is the significance of that? For his part, Harry wouldn't
be surprised if the guard, with this kind of baiting on the one
hand and blatantly sucking up to me on the other, wasn't trying
to drive a wedge between us. It's probably to his advantage.
Yes, it may sound strange to me. The question is, can we exclude
it? Can we safely exclude it? No, says Harry, absolutely not. He
might be a special agent, but maybe he has his own agenda too.
Who's to say? Harry says we have to keep our eyes peeled. We
have to evaluate the situation daily or, better still, hourly! It's of
the utmost importance. Wouldn't it be terrible after all this time
in the basement to let ourselves be outsmarted? By a newcomer?
Harry and me? Us?

106

The guard might not be withholding information simply because it's to his own advantage. Who's to say he's not doing it to see how well we hold up under pressure? Because, Harry whispers in the darkness near the crushers, let's not beat about the bush, whether he's a special agent or not, the organization must have briefed him, no two ways about it. And not just regarding the situation outside. That's why he doesn't ask about the last resident or the residents who have disappeared and it's why he doesn't bat an eyelid about not seeing a single motor vehicle in a basement car park. Harry repeats that, in the same situation, he would find that last bit very weird and I would too, of course, for Christ's sake. But not the guard. He's not bothered because he knows a lot more about what's going on here than we do. I can take that as read, Harry says. And his sucking up to me might not be blatant, no, maybe it's not blatant, it's more cunning than that. I should just think about those porcelain figurines of his if I don't believe him. What a trick! It's clear that the guard is trying to win my confidence. And according to Harry that's not just to set us against each other. At the same time the guard wants to wheedle as much out of us as he can, anything that might be useful, anything that increases his headstart. Because that's how I should see it. That's how Harry sees it. With the hair of his moustache brushing the top of my ear, he asks if I'm aware of just how scarce positions in the elite are? We mustn't lose sight of that. Do I hear him?

107

It all comes down to one thing, Harry says: us not knowing who this bloke really is. We haven't got a clue. And the guard might have convinced me that he's the second-to-last in a family of seven boys and that his father worked in the mines for forty years, but so what? What's that tell us about him? That he's learnt to take a back seat? To be obedient? A hard worker? Is that what we're supposed to deduce from his words? No bloody idea. We don't even know if he's speaking the truth. We don't know him. We only know one thing: he's not stupid. He's not stupid and he's a competitor. Let's not forget that, for crying out loud. He's a guard, he'll back us up if necessary. Harry doesn't doubt that, he credits him with that much of a sense of honour. But he's also a competitor trying to coax as much out of us as he can, anything that can improve his already advantageous position and bring him closer to his goal. He'll shrink at nothing. And I might be cautious, of course I'm cautious, that goes without saying, but no matter how cautious I am, it's difficult to prevent him from picking up little titbits of information the moment I relax. The guard doesn't try it on with Harry. And with good fucking reason. He knows he won't get anywhere. Harry's not giving anything away, do I understand that? And do I also understand that the guard wouldn't mind a position in the elite either? He might be a special agent, who's to say, but he still has to feed his face out of the same tins as Harry and me. And like the two of us, Harry says, he's still locked up the whole God-awful day in this godforsaken hole. Don't I think that, just like us, the guard wants something else? Fresh air? Some greenery? Do I think he'd turn his nose up at a chance to guard Mr Van der Burg-Zethoven's white villa? Do I think he'd look the other way if Mr Van der Burg-Zethoven's fiancée was stretched out on a white sofa in front of the window stroking her hairless pussy? Harry's just giving an example. And can we blame the guard? He'd be an idiot if it was any other way. No, we understand completely. But not at our expense. Not Harry's and mine. No way. The guard will have to get up earlier in the morning if he thinks he can steal all the credit by playing us off one against each other while he acts the innocent. The credit we, Harry and I and no-one else, have earned twice over, more. Because that's what it comes down to. That's what we have to keep in the forefront of our mind every second of every day, says Harry. The positions are limited, don't forget. The competition is murderous.

108

Do I know what suddenly occurred to him today? Do I know what's been on his mind all afternoon? The resident. The man on 29, the last resident. It's like this. We, Harry and me, don't need the guard's help: for us that's as clear as crystal and maybe the organization will see it that way soon too. We function just fine shut off from the world and whether they're big or little, fat or thin, we don't need any blacks down here helping us. But there's also a flipside to this miserable affair. A side that far surpasses the guard's underhand interests . . .

I hear Harry pacing to and fro in the pitch darkness, a metre or two in front of my feet, short lengths; the grit under his shoes crunches as he turns. I wonder how he manages to keep his orientation, if he'll soon bump into the crusher or, worse, my forehead or knees.

It is unacceptable, Harry says, that the client's interests should suffer in any way at all because of the secret ambitions of a clown like the guard. That is fundamentally wrong; it goes against everything the organization stands for. The whole point of all this is the client's security, which is under serious and acute threat. That's why the organization's sent the guard. And what is a guard's number one priority? For all guards, wherever they're stationed, irrespective of any ambitions they might harbour? Harry is going to tell me: the client. It's the client who digs deep into his pocket for our special services, the client who is our priority, the client and no-one else. We, as guards, as individuals, do not actually exist. We live for the client. Anyway, says Harry, how long have we been locked up in this basement now? How long without faltering even once? Harry and me, us? I know it better than he does, says Harry, no, he doesn't have to tell me. If we, with our service record, can't lay claim to a pillowcase or a flannel of our own, to give an example, then we at least have the right to information that is crucial to the protection of our client? Surely?

109

What do I think about it? Surely I must agree with him that the situation is absurd. We're stuck here like sitting ducks. And by "we" Harry doesn't just mean him and me but, more than anyone else, the last resident too. At the mercy of the pettiness and disgusting lack of professionalism of a fellow guard, who is also putting his own safety at risk in the process. Like some kind of suicide bomber who'll stop at nothing to reach his goal. An insult to our profession and a personal humiliation for both of us because isn't it so that, by consistently withholding information, the guard is constantly laughing in our faces? I should just stop and consider it from a fresh perspective. After a while things get muddled of course. After a while the guard starts thinking he's got a clear playing field, that there's nothing stopping him. If I look at the situation from a fresh perspective, I'll come to the same conclusion. I can take that from Harry. There's just no other option. We have to intervene. We can't let this state of affairs carry on any longer. What would the organization require us to do? Just keep plodding along? Do I know what it is? We misjudged things. We wanted to prove our independence by not asking the guard any questions and carrying on with our work as if he's not even here. It hasn't helped. Harry doesn't exclude the possibility that the guard, if he really is an agent with honourable intentions, is waiting for the exact opposite: initiative. Engagement. If he's a good agent, he'll understand our intervention

151

perfectly and value it. He won't report it as a sign of weakness or stress. He'll speak of dedication, praising us for our bold action, while fully understanding our initial reticence. That's how Harry sees it. And if the guard isn't honourable, we'll have to come up with something to make him better his ways. We no longer have any choice.

110

"A what?"

"An agent," Harry repeats. "Someone who's been dispatched on a special mission. In this case, a secret mission."

Just now, when I caught a glimpse of the guard through the crack, he was sitting on the side of my bed, lower arms on his knees. Slightly surprised, but imperturbable, he looked at the corner with the washbasin, where Harry had presumably taken up position. Harry thought he should interrogate the guard himself, to impress the seriousness of the situation on him from the start. We had no time to lose. I'm sitting on the chair outside the bunkroom door; someone has to keep watch. All ears, I stare absent-mindedly into the middle of the basement.

After a silence the guard says, almost whispering, "I don't think so. But if I was an agent on a secret mission, I obviously wouldn't be allowed to talk about it. The organization would have forbidden it. A guard is obliged to respect the rules."

"True," Harry says. "But you could say whether or not you've been given a special mission, without letting slip what that mission entails."

"I understand that," the guard says.

"It's in the interest of the resident."

"The resident?"

"The last resident, on 29. You sharing your information with us is in his interest. You know that his security is under threat. That's why you're here. He's the first priority, for you as a guard."

"I don't think I'm an agent. I'm a guard."

"Sometimes you can be both."

"An agent and a guard?"

Harry doesn't deem this question worthy of an answer. Either that or he nods.

"What kind of secret mission would I have if I had one?"

"One you'd know all about."

"What do you think?"

"No idea. Actually, it's not important. What's important is you sharing your information with us."

"Don't you want to tell me what you think?"

"I told you, I don't know. I'm not a special agent." Harry's voice betrays the difficulty he's having trying to control himself.

"And you're sure they exist, these agents?"

"Maybe you can tell me."

"Yes," the guard says with conviction. "I think they do exist. In secret."

"Are you one?"

"No. I'm a guard."

"You're a guard who's putting his own life at risk. Do you realize that?"

"It's better," the guard says after a while, "to banish bad thoughts from your mind and only think about good things."

"Are you taking the piss?"

I think I can hear Harry's breathing.

153

"You don't sound very friendly."

"Maybe you're not acting like a good colleague. You're not just endangering yourself but also the resident, more than anyone else, and Michel and me. Not a very good colleague, in other words, and anything but professional."

"Michel?"

"Yes. Michel and me too. Just like at your previous post. If we can believe your stories at least."

"What do you mean by that?"

"That I, for starters, don't believe your story. And if those porcelain figurines existed, you also put your previous colleague in danger by going to talk to him . . ."

The guard is apparently dumbstruck, horrified.

The silence presses on my chest, pinning me to the spot.

"Only twice," I finally hear. Words that float out calmly on the deep vibrations of his voice box. "I shouldn't have done it. I thought he was my friend."

111

After making sure the guard is asleep, Harry takes me by the arm. In the darkness between Garages 34 and 35 he asks what has happened in the last few hours. While I was asleep, the guard completely ignored him, as if he didn't exist. Harry claims that the whole situation suits the guard down to the ground. His feigned indignation about our accusation gives him the ideal excuse for not saying another word. If he hadn't known already, he now realizes what an enormous advantage he's at. Harry says we're facing a difficult, if not impossible task. I remark that I didn't notice any great difference from before. Maybe the guard was a little quieter, a bit more introspective, but he talked. Not about the issue, that was a subject he avoided. Just a bit of chit-chat now and then. I got the impression, I say, that he was trying to reassure me. Reassure you, Harry repeats softly. That was my impression, I say, yes. I say that I assumed he wanted to let me know that he didn't mind and that I didn't need to feel bad about it. That he understood me telling you his story. Something like that . . . Harry keeps quiet. It's as if he's dissolved into darkness. Just when I'm convinced that he must have heard something somewhere else in the basement, the soles of his shoes crunch as he turns.

112

Is he speaking loud enough? It really is true and there's no need for me to worry. After all, it's a test; somehow, it's a test. But we're one step ahead. It won't be easy. We'll have to act hon-ourably. I can leave it to him. Am I listening? From out of nowhere, Harry presses his chest against me. He says everything will turn out well. He hugs me. Our caps bump and turn. I smell walnut. Everything will work out. He pushes me away and tells me I'll see. He squeezes my shoulders and talks at me. I don't need to worry, not for a second. Of course the guard would answer me that he doesn't use flannels. The bastard. What did I expect? Of course he'd say he washes himself with his hands. His answer doesn't surprise Harry in the least. Am I listening, do I understand? Have I given the situation enough thought? How long we've been here in the basement together, all the things we've been through. He doesn't have to tell me that. No flannel! Harry heard us, me and the guard, he clearly heard us talking again. But that was last night. Water under the bridge. No flannel! The black shit. He'd do better to use one. Stinks to high heaven. Terrible. Isn't it terrible? The way he manipulates and uses us. Not an ounce of respect. No, guys like him never have any. They rabbit on about it the whole time, sure – respect this, respect that – but when it comes down to it . . . It makes your skin crawl. It's all behind us now. It's in the past. We have to trust each other. We're being put to the test, but it's never simple. There's no time left. We mustn't neglect our duty. I needn't worry. As long as we keep our faith in each other, we're untouchable. Neither of us can lose sight of that. I have to remember that. I have to keep it in mind. We've earned our place in the elite. Him and me. We have to do what's expected of us. Sometimes life is simple. Sometimes life taps you on the shoulder and takes you by the hand. Do I hear him? Harry presses up against me. His breast expands and contracts. It will all work out. I can leave it to Harry. He hugs me. I'll see.

113

I let the Flock slip out of my hand and push the lowest button on my wristwatch to turn off the alarm. I stay lying on the mattress for a couple of minutes with my eyes open. Images that have visited me constantly for the last five hours sink slowly to the bottom of my clearing consciousness. I take my pistol, swing my legs over the side of the bed, and push myself up off the metal frame. I take two or three steps in the dark, put the barrel against the light switch and push.

It's as if I can tell that something's not normal from the mirror, from the reflection of my face, but my face is the same as any other day. It's not my face, I realize that at once, it's not me.

It's the room.

Slowly I turn around. I'm standing in front of an empty floor.

I wave my arm cautiously and feel no resistance where the table used to be. It feels like I'm moving my arm straight through it, that's how hard it is for me to believe my eyes. I have never seen the room without the table: it was already here when I arrived, right in this spot. A cheap garden table with grey weathered planks. Now it's gone.

I wash my face, clean my teeth, rinse out my mouth, dress quickly and brush my uniform. Outside I wait at the bunkroom door. Harry and the guard must be near the entrance. I scan the sides of the basement, searching for a blur of movement. I can't see their legs or feet anywhere. I can't see the table anywhere either. After a while, I feel the seat of the chair. Cold.

I judge it better to stay here for the time being. It's better for me to keep still and wait.

What reason could they have had for moving the table out of the bunkroom? And why do it when I was asleep?

The buzzing of the middle fluorescent light builds up. While I'm looking at it, the tube dies with a flash and a pop. A black hole drops into the middle of the basement as if that part of the ceiling has collapsed.

"I'll replace that straight away," Harry says. "We've still got

157

plenty of spares." He is coming out of the storeroom. He pulls the door shut behind him and locks it. His jacket is folded neatly and draped over his forearm. He must have removed the key from the pocket of my trousers while I was asleep. Ever since I've been stationed here, it has been my responsibility to inspect the storeroom twice a day, and especially the ammunition. That's why I always have the key in my pocket.

114

As if he's heading out for the evening or has just come back, that's how his jacket is draped over his arm. The storeroom key disappears in his trouser pocket. He's in a cheerful mood. It is so peculiar to see Harry emerging from the storeroom with his jacket draped over his arm that I don't recognize him, even though it's patently obvious it's Harry. It's as if I am now seeing him for the first time.

He's hot, his shirt is wet with sweat. Not just under the arms, but around the neck and on the back too. An hour before washing it, I'll rub liquid soap into those patches, the way I always do the collars. If you saturate the cotton with soap, you can hardly see or smell the sweat stains afterwards.

Harry sits down on the chair, laying the jacket over his legs. Evidently he wants to calmly finish the count before withdrawing to the bunkroom. I sit down on the stool and pull the Flock 28 out of my holster, push in the magazine catch and let the cartridge clip slide out of the butt. I count in silence. Fifteen. I wait for Harry, for the result of his inspection. His Flock stays on his hip. When he makes no move to count his cartridges, I remember the table. Harry says the table is in the storeroom, it's more use there. After a short silence in which I wait for an explanation, he says blandly that I won't need to do any timing for a while. He taps his watch with a long fingernail. It won't be necessary. He's alluding to the guard's long visits to the toilet, although the really long visits generally take place just after he wakes up. What's more, I only time them in the day, when there are three of us.

We wait for the guard for a while, but then Harry tugs his tie loose and stands up. I say good night.

"Keep your eyes peeled," he says.

"I will."

"Maybe," Harry says, "it would be better if you took up position outside the storeroom. Near the door. You never know with these guys. They're slow, but they're built like gorillas."

115

A sledgehammer blow of his fist, which won't let itself be stopped by a bit of compacted sawdust between two sheets of grey veneer. I constantly expect that first, pounding smash on the door. Almost an hour has passed in nerve-wracking silence.

The cylinder of the lock prevents me looking in. I can't see any light under the door.

A wild cat leaping up against the bars, spitting frothy saliva. I pass the pistol to my left hand to wipe the sweat off my palm. Long curving fangs clamped on the unyielding iron for hours.

Forehead and face a bloody lump of raw meat. Caged beasts. Their nature.

An hour later I'm calmer. I lean back with my head against the wall so that I will pick up the least little vibration on the other side. I still have all the time in the world to get wound up. The guard is probably asleep.

It's just a coincidence he's not snoring tonight.

With my heart in my throat I slowly push the toilet door open. Empty. The seat is up. I return immediately.

I do two inspection rounds, each time hurrying back to the storeroom door. I seek out the grey rectangle from a great distance, my eyes homing in on it. I am attached by a line and slowly reeled in.

I cough, by chance, then deliberately. I cough and listen. It's a small room and it's quiet. If the guard is awake, he now knows I'm here. He'll understand I'm on guard here and not at the bunkroom. I can hear him easily, even if he whispers.

I scratch with my nails. As if lightly tickling the door.

He knows I don't want to wake anyone up.

Does he think, having just woken, that he's heard a mouse? A mouse?

I clear my throat. I recognize my voice in the sound.

Is he sleeping on the table?

Is he sitting in the corner between the rations and the ammunition, on the concrete ledge? He has wrapped his arms around his legs. Is he thinking of his old dad, bent over in a mineshaft? Is he trying to grasp how long forty years is?

He thinks, I have to keep quiet.

He sits in a corner and waits for his time to come.

The convenience of only having one possibility. The advantage.

He thinks, this is my chance.

He thinks, if I keep quiet, sooner or later he'll open the door and then I'll grab the little runt by the throat and squeeze it tight before he can let out a peep.

116

He hangs his cap over his jacket on the hook on the wall. The door is wide open. He lingers by the foot of the bed. After twenty-four hours almost everything is back to how it was before. We sleep either side of midnight, the best hours. I've scrubbed the smell of the guard's body out of the linen with my fists. I push my nose into the pillow and sniff. I want to keep smelling this all night: liquid soap, no matter how artificial or industrial the perfume. I'll be able to drift off into a deep sleep again without any trouble. I'll be able to dream calm dreams and wake up refreshed. It's like the old days. The guard isn't here. He has never been here. We're guarding the building alone again. It's the first time since he suddenly appeared. Harry spits on his hand. Twice. He's angry, I feel that at once. It hurts, but of course his anger isn't directed at me. "A few more days," he growls in my ear. "When he's hungry enough, he'll start to talk. We can count on it." He's angry. I hold tight, but he's angry about the guard and all the things he's keeping secret. Harry laughs with anger, saying they can't touch us. He is rough and presses down on me with all his weight, but that has nothing to do with me.

117

Harry slips in for the interrogation. He holds the Flock at the ready, close to his cheek, turns the key in the lock, opens the door no wider than necessary and shuffles in sideways, flicking the light on and immediately closing the door behind him.

After three days he no longer greets the guard.

No more, "You know what we want to hear." Or, "Are you ready for some more?" Or, "Shall I undo the gag so you can get it off your chest?" Or, "Come on, matey, don't be shy."

After three days Harry goes back to eating his meals outside, next to me.

The time Harry spends in the storeroom now passes in almost constant silence. As if he's keeping vigil at a relative's deathbed: a question of hours.

Now and then I jump from the sound of a blow striking home and Harry screaming that the guard has to stop, that he has to stop his little games, that it's for his own good, begging him to once, just once, think of the resident, the client after all, who doesn't know what's hanging over his head, and what kind of gutless guard is he anyway? As long as he doesn't think someone's going to clean up after him. He can just lie there in his own filth. It's either talk or stay lying there like that, it's either stay lying there like that or eat and drink, and what's it going to be?

Harry says that the guard is lying on the table. He's sacrificed his sheet, tearing it up into strips. He says he tied the guard up straight away and since then he hasn't made a single attempt to get loose. He asks me if I know why. He'll tell me: it's his guilty conscience eating away at him.

118

One morning Harry appears in his grey vest with his jacket, shirt and tie draped over his arm. Drenched in sweat and with his pale, freckled shoulders drooping, he locks the storeroom door and slips the key into his trouser pocket. He scratches the hair on his throat irritably, removes his cap, then puts it back on at the correct angle.

"It's hard," Harry says after catching his breath on the chair. "It's a hard, merciless test and you and me, we just have to get through it. It's about determination, Michel. For the sake of that one human life above us. For the sake of his security."

He fills his mouth with bottled water and shakes his head gently while swallowing it in two gulps. "If the guard's an agent, he's a kind of agent we could never have suspected. A completely new kind, for insane fucking missions they reserve for niggers."

119

Although it's the middle of my sleep, I'm immediately awake, as if I've been lying here for three hours with my eyes closed waiting for this scream. Now that it's come, I'm hardly surprised. It is the first sound from the guard in six days.

He screams that he doesn't know a thing about a last resident. I hear it word for word.

He doesn't scream aimlessly, this is no uncontrolled eruption. His scream has a purpose. His voice and the way it's raised tell us that this first time will also be the last time. His contribution is once only and definitive. He won't be adding anything else. It's over and out.

I am staring into the darkness when Harry comes into the bunkroom and switches on the light. He paces back and forth from the door to the washbasin, keeping it up for a couple of minutes. With the table gone, his steps ring in the small room.

"Did you hear what he said?" Harry asks. "One sentence. That's enough. He gave himself away from the word go. Did you hear it? The last resident? He claims he doesn't have a clue. Yeah, that makes it obvious, doesn't it? The last resident is the *reason* for his posting! Are we really supposed to believe the organization hasn't informed him about the *reason* for his posting? If he knows anything at all, then surely that there's only one left, one single resident who's in great danger, enough danger for three instead of two guards."

Later – I've washed and dressed and am sitting on the stool next to the door even though I have almost an hour left in which to rest – Harry says he needs my help. From now on we have to keep the guard awake the whole time. If we also keep him awake in the hours that Harry's asleep, then we'll manage it. No doubt about it. He'll definitely snap.

I have to go into the storeroom with him, Harry says. There's something he needs to show me, a trick. The way he does it.

120

With the Flock up near my cheek I follow Harry into the darkness, creeping into the stench, a musty cocktail I can't break down into its constituent elements. Urine, in any case, stale urine. I feel my eyes watering and press back against the wall. I shut out the idea that this foul air is entering my lungs, settling in soft tissue, contaminating my body with horrific complaints that will only reveal themselves after an incubation period, starting with small, unmistakable signs: itching, subcutaneous blisters, blurred vision, blood-streaked stools, fungal infections. I am firmly convinced that it is not the absence of electric light, but the unutterable stench that is responsible for the darkness in the storeroom.

Once Harry has locked the door and turned on the light, I am able, after an intense bout of blinking, to see again. I don't know what reaches my retina first. The boxes. Sideways. Without casting a conscious glance in that direction, I see that the ammunition on the shelves hasn't been touched. The boxes stand in rank, exactly as during my last inspection. There's no time for this vague consolation, because my brain is faced with the task of deciphering what the table, in the middle of the room, is presenting me with. Limbs, spread slightly, and bound to the planks by the white cotton tentacles of a powerful creature that is concealed under the table and reaching up through the cracks. The limbs are defenceless and naked and the planks are no longer grey, but black, saturated as if after a cloudburst. The guard isn't wearing his uniform: I don't see any blue anywhere, I don't see any underwear. His large feet are angled outwards. One of his hands is turned up, his right. In the pale palm I see dead insects, worms, grubs. His mouth is fixed in a grin by the grimy gag. His eyes are closed; he's already sound asleep. Exhausted from his scream. No, not grubs. Gradations of the rosy colour have spread all over his immense black body. It's on his face, his penis, his calves, the soles of his feet. I screw my eyes up out of instinctive revulsion. He is covered with it; the guard is no longer entirely black. The new colour has soaked into the tentacles close to the wet wood. The marks on the white stripes merge into pale brown. His penis, as thick as a smoked sausage, is resting on a swollen, pitch-black pouch and nestling against the inside of his thigh. Under a wreath of knobs of hair. He is circumcised, no, the foreskin has been pulled back, bunched up and wrinkled against the edge of the glans as if he has just had an erection. There is plenty of pink on the glans, on the pouch, on the shaft. This is what I see in a few seconds. It's not grubs, it's cuts. It is bulging flesh: pink, whitish pink, grey and purplish red. A lot of yellow too. I see greenish yellow. I smell stale urine and suppurating flesh. I concentrate on the flat underside of his big toe, close by, to suppress the rising nausea. The pale, flat underside of his big toe. Miraculously spared. Or used as a lever to stretch the sole of his foot.

121

This is what I see in a couple of seconds. With these hundreds of colourful bulges, his body looks like it's engaged in a horrific struggle, molecular warfare, blossoming flesh erupting through his old skin. He's undergoing a metamorphosis.

Harry goes over to the table and bends over the guard's head. He says that for two days now he's been too bloody-minded to open his eyes so that he can never be sure if the guard's awake or not and has to keep at it the whole time.

From close by, Harry stares at the shining eyelids. Their noses are almost touching when he bursts out screaming, "Yes, Michel, Mr Sensitive is taunting us!" Harry yells each word separately, as hard as his lungs and vocal chords can manage and all in the same tone.

Suddenly, without drawing my attention to it, Harry is holding a tool in his hand. I recognize the transparent, light-blue plastic of our water bottles. It surrounds his fist. It's the bottom of a bottle. A short blade is protruding from this protective covering. The paring knife.

He says, "This is how I do it."

Harry emphasizes the "I". He does it like this. He's giving me a tip, not an order. If I can find a better way, he'd be glad to hear it.

At first, Harry explains, he thought he had to nick him in a new spot every time. He did it more or less every ten minutes, it made sure the black bastard paid attention. Eventually, however, he discovered by chance that cutting open old wounds is more effective. Generally he observes a reaction over his whole body. A bit like a cow that's bumped an electric fence. He asks if I understand him. He still needs to keep nicking him in new places as well because it takes a while before the wound is infected enough to give his lordship a good shake. As strange as it sounds, Harry says, I'll need to lay in a supply. The simplest, he's found, is to alternate every ten minutes: new, old. But I'll find out myself. The situation is constantly changing.

Harry studies the guard's body. On the side above a knee he finds what he was looking for. He indicates a position on the other side of the table that will give me a good view of the procedure. When he pulls the blunt paring knife forcefully over the swelling, green fluid splats out against the light-blue plastic. The intense contraction in the guard's arms and legs keeps up for quite a while. "No two ways about it," Harry says. "He's awake now."

Outside, at the bunkroom door, before going to sleep, Harry urges me not to forget one thing. The guard is silent because he knows something. If he didn't know anything, or if he wasn't an agent, he would have made something up long ago.

122

A half-hour passes. The guard's breathing is regular; he's probably sleeping deeply. I'm sitting on the concrete ledge in the corner between the rations and the ammunition and staring at the stains on the ground. The resident is our priority. He is my priority. I repeat that to myself.

I hear mumbling. The guard has opened his eyes and turned his head towards me. He is looking for me and as soon as I stand up and come into his field of vision, his deep voice sounds again, incomprehensible because of the gag.

Is it because I've given him a respite of half an hour that he is now willing to talk?

The material is damp. The hard double knot is difficult to loosen. The dark eyes are fixed on me constantly. When I carefully remove the strip, from one corner of his mouth and then the other, he tries immediately to say something, but this time it's his cramped tongue that's getting in the way. A few seconds later I understand the word he is struggling to pronounce.

"Friend."

A strange smile appears on his face. It's a smile that doesn't go with the state he's in.

What makes him think I'm his friend? How could I be his friend? What kind of conceit is that, laying claim to someone's friendship just because they were polite to you?

"I'm not your friend."

I ask if he can hear me.

I am surprised by the sound of my voice in the storeroom.

The guard's smile gets bigger, he whispers, "My friend."

He thinks, this is my last chance. He thinks, I'll wind this gutless good-for-nothing around my little finger. I'll flash him my most beautiful smile. I'll call him my friend. He's got no back-bone. Piece of cake. He fell for those porcelain figurines too, of course. I'll grin in his face and throw him off balance. If I just lie on my back like a dog and look at him faithfully with big eyes, he'll pat me on the stomach.

"Have you got something to say?"

The guard lies on the table, relaxed and shameless, smiling his stupid smile.

He doesn't think, when it comes down to it, Michel is a guard too. I mustn't be blinded by his good manners. If I don't immediately stop grinning, and if I'm stupid enough to insult him again by making another wild claim of friendship, I'll set him off. He might hesitate, but once the faltering knife has been lubricated by the rising blood, he'll carve to the bone.

123

Two days later, five o'clock in the afternoon, Harry opens the storeroom door and asks if I would like to come in. He walks around the table and says I should feel the guard's pulse. With the tip of my middle finger on a small, untouched patch of skin, I look at the turned head, the closed eyes, the crack between the dry, fleshy lips. There is a silence without any perceptible movement: three men under a bulb in a storeroom. Like a canvas by a seventeenth-century master, captured in the light.

124

Harry and I take small, jolting, sideways steps. We're not synchronizing and that makes carrying him even more difficult.

Sometimes the guard's ankles are almost ripped out of my hands. We should count – one-two, one-two – but now we're in the middle of it and making progress, we muddle along through the basement. Occasionally his buttocks drag over the concrete.

"The resident," Harry pants, "has paid for his security . . . If we want to prove our dedication . . . We have to go to any lengths . . . If we want to have a chance . . . We have to get him . . . Thanks to this bastard we're in the dark . . . It's up to us now . . . We have to save him."

"Save him?"

Harry nods confidently. "We'll bring him down to the basement . . . In the storeroom . . . One of us on the door at all times . . . He has to be spared . . . One human life, Michel . . . By saving one human life, we save humanity."

We drag the guard over the ground on the curve of his hipbone. We don't have any strength left. In the middle of the basement, we let his trunk and legs flop to the ground and slump down next to him. The very thought of leaving this basement! The concept is too enormous, it pushes out against the inside of my burning head, pressure on the back of my eyes.

"You and me," Harry says a little later. "No-one can match us." He grins over his shoulder, waiting for me to smile back. "But this job first. Come on, we have to hurry."

Again I wrap the guard's torn vest around my hands. I tell Harry that we have to count, moving in time to make it less of a load.

"I've got a better idea." Harry removes the big, soiled shirt he has been wearing like a bib with the sleeves tied around his neck. He passes one of the guard's hands to me and grips the other wrist tightly. We set our feet firmly on the ground and throw our weight into the struggle. Stretching the arms changes the pressures in his organs and bubbles of gas escape from the lower body, one after the other, as if our quick backwards steps are pulling a string of marbles out of his intestines.

We cover a good fifty metres without stopping. At the entrance to the narrow space between Garages 34 and 35 we let go. The back of the guard's head cracks down on the concrete.

"Somehow we'll have to get him up onto my shoulders," Harry says. "Otherwise we'll never get him over the edge."

I'm glad of the darkness near the crushers, glad that, during the struggle that ensues, the growling and the raging, the stench and the filth, I don't have to see what I'm touching, what I'm pressing my cheek against, which body part I'm supporting with the top of my head. Or how Harry's coping with the crotch around his neck.

I hear it rustle as it falls, shorter than a moment. In the absence of a visual denouement, the abrupt release from the heavy weight makes me feel like I'm floating a couple of centimetres above the ground. The impact is a cacophony: empty tins shoot off in all directions, rolling for metres in the steel container. When the very last sound has died out – clearly a round tin which, after defining ever-decreasing circles, produced a crescendo by spinning around its centre of gravity – I hear Harry flick a switch on the control panel. There is no electricity to start the motor, we know that, but Harry still messes around with the buttons and, as I'm thinking, it's impossible, it can't be, after all this time the crusher can't have even a remnant of hydraulic pressure left, generated by one of the servants for God's sake, and as Arthur appears in my mind's eye, Arthur from the Poborskis on 39, Arthur in his dark-blue dustcoat, there is a click and the wall slides slowly over the floor, reaching the first tin, the second, sweeping the rattling tins into a pile, pushing the guard

172

along too, and, as I'm thinking, now the slide is going to stop, now it's run out, now it's too heavy, I hear the internal rumbling increase and, just before the crusher dies on us, a sound like a rubbish bag popping in the depths of the container.

THREE

125

We're walking to the lifts. It is inconceivable that we're doing this. Residents, visitors, staff: Harry and I walk towards them. The only entrance to the building, a solution that has been forced upon us. Forty luxurious floors, virtually forgotten, rise above us in full glory. We've never seen so much as a glimpse of them! It is inconceivable that we're doing this. With the intention of leaving the basement, Harry and me! And yet we're walking to the lifts. Our exit. The basement, where we live, will become a basement again, an empty car park. With each step, I'm dreaming. My pulse pounds in my temples; I can feel it shaking my head. The excitement. As if the resident has been hiding in one of the lifts since the exodus. Harry and I have finally discovered him, soon we'll meet him. I see the distance growing smaller and know that it is inconceivable. I try to remember what Harry has said about the man, the man we have to save. I get no further than a shaven head and black clothes. A few metres before the lifts we stop and stare silently at the smooth grey doors, impassive in their steel frames. Everything has been an exercise, preparation. Now it's time for it to really start.

126

The service lift, a little larger than the other two, is the only one with double doors that meet in the middle. Harry sends me to the staff storage cupboard for two barrels of liquid soap. When I come back, I see him working at the rubber. He's used the paring knife to gouge out a notch. He digs at it and pulls pieces and long black strips out of the seal.

"Shall I get two more? There's another two." I nod at the fifteen-litre barrels.

Harry's blank face bursts into a smile. He winks to show his appreciation. "Hurry."

A little later we're standing next to the double doors facing each other with our fingertips in the crack Harry has opened up. We both slide a foot past the halfway mark, crossing our legs. We puff up our cheeks. We form a strange but completely symmetrical figure, Harry and me, guards.

A long, hopeless period of strain and exertion follows. But once we've achieved an opening of about ten centimetres, the sliding doors suddenly capitulate and retract mechanically. Inside the lift, the light flicks on, giving me the fright of my life. Momentarily blinded, I automatically let go. It's as if we've tugged on a living creature and woken it, in God knows what kind of mood.

"Quick," Harry says.

We slide the barrels into position. Thirty kilos on the left, thirty on the right. They do a good job of cushioning the blows of the sliding doors, which keep on wanting to close again. We stand there with our hands on our hips, like road workers looking at the new asphalt.

"Do you think the lift still works?"

Harry nods, surprised by my question. "Of course, look." He takes a couple of steps back and points at the small red light set into the top of the frame. "If the light's gone back on here, it will be working on the other floors too. Try it, if you like. But not me. I'm not taking the lift, Michel. I don't know what's waiting for us. Do you know what's happened up there? Have you ever been there? I know I haven't. If we use the lift, we'll have pretty little lights announcing our arrival. Don't you think?"

I feel the heaviness in my exhausted shoulders. I have to think faster, I have to stay awake. There's only one absolute certainty and that certainty is called a Flock 28 and it's strapped to my hip. Everything else must at all times be appraised. Gauged. Sniffed out. Fortunately Harry is experienced. Together we can't be outsmarted. I disappoint him, but he doesn't hold it against me.

Harry steps tentatively into the lift, saying that Arthur once told him about stairs that run down past the staff apartments to the ground floor.

I can hardly believe it. Not what he's said about the stairs, but his unexpectedly mentioning Arthur's name when I was thinking about him less than ten minutes ago. How strange it is after such a long time, even though it's nothing special.

127

Harry doesn't need to ask me for the chair. He only needs to glance up at the hatch in the ceiling of the lift cabin. He moves over under the hatch to study it carefully, looking straight up with his head tipped so far back that his mouth hangs open.

"In and out," he says, stepping up onto the chair. "We have to do it as fast as possible, not staying a minute longer than necessary. Upstairs is forbidden territory. But we're both going, Michel, there's no alternative. The alternative is very dicey. If something happened to one of us, preventing him from coming back, what would the other do then?"

I assume he means it as a rhetorical question, but either way, I try not to think about it. First things first, starting with the little things in my immediate vicinity that demand my attention.

Harry uses the paring knife to scratch away the dirt and paint. The hatch has almost certainly never been used. He keeps the base of his clenched fist close to it as if waiting for a signal. One firm blow makes the hatch pop up before falling back with a much louder clang. Above the cabin we hear the noise echo shrilly in the confined space, fading away and surging back, up and down the interminable shaft.

To climb up through the hatch we'll need the table.

128

Harry shines the guard's torch up the shaft. Its beam shows us the steel lift cables and a black hole where they dissolve in the distance, creating an illusion of us holding long, fist-thick bars that stick up from the roof of the cabin. Harry shines the light back down at our feet to make sure we don't stumble over anything. The shaft smells like a building site. It has never been subjected to any air but its own.

We assume the same positions as before. We're halfway up to the ground floor, tugging on the doors at head height. I feel like I'm doing permanent damage to my back, muscles and joints. This time no mechanism comes to our aid but the resistance does drop off noticeably after about ten centimetres. The light is dim, the polished stone floor gleams faintly. Finally there is no more resistance and the door stays open of its own accord; we gape with surprise for a moment and only then bend our knees to drop below the opening. My shirt is soaked, stretched over my skin like a chamois. Harry turns off the torch.

Minutes pass.

Together we peer over the edge. I feel a draught on my eyeballs. The slight gleam on the floor is the result of artificial lighting, tucked away somewhere to the right. We clamber up out of the shaft, making so much racket that I feel like they're only holding their fire out of pity.

One behind the other, we creep along the wall, avoiding the

open space like rodents. I don't think Harry knows where we have to go. There were two possibilities. We've gone left. Into the darkness.

129

I hear Harry's hand sliding over the stone skirting. If the entrance to the stairwell is on the right next to the lift, we'll only discover it after covering the entire perimeter of the ground floor on our knees and elbows, more or less the distance of our basement inspection round.

After what I imagine to be about thirty metres, we still haven't found anything. After another five, I tap Harry on the calf. He stops immediately, lying there as if he's dead.

I crawl up next to him and feel for his head and ear, which I move my mouth close to. I whisper that we should turn back, telling him that it looks like the door is located to the right of the lifts.

"Right," Harry says into my ear in turn, "is towards the front of the building. The staff apartments are probably at the back. That sounds logical to me. Residents at the front, servants at the back. What do you think?"

Harry isn't being cynical, he waits for my answer. And while I answer, I feel that I'm right. We can, after all, save ourselves an awful lot of misery by going back first to make sure. In my experience stairwells and lift shafts are built close together.

I am now crawling in front and keeping up a good speed.

We creep past the yawning lift doors. The indirect artificial light seems to increase a little in strength, shining along a wall. I see the bottom of an ornate frame, not much more than a shadow really, a jagged edge dissolving into darkness. As we get closer to the light, I am able to make out the veins in the light marble floor. The skirting stops. I feel a corner and, around it and set back a few metres, I see light under a door. Nothing on the sides, but at the bottom the gap is so big that I can see in past the door: the floor carries on and the reflection of another door is floating in the gleam.

I crawl into the niche. Harry follows me. Together we stand up. The handle is on Harry's side. Slowly he pushes the door open. When he's seen enough, he turns to me and whispers, "Toilets."

The emergency lighting is on and nothing like the emergency lighting in the basement. It's a series of recessed wall and ceiling lights that would be invisible when turned off. Toilets on the ground floor where nobody ever comes. On the dark washstand a pile of folded towels is waiting next to the washbasin; the wicker basket is empty. Our uniforms look good in the large, tinted mirror. Two doors with, behind each one, the same dark washstand, the washbasin, the towels and the empty wicker basket. Wooden coat hangers in a built-in cupboard. A real painting on the wall: flowers with thick daubs of paint, as thick as the flowers themselves. Under the painting, a tall, two-person sofa with old-rose upholstery, armrests and a white varnished back.

Harry stands still in a cubicle and looks into the toilet bowl for a long time with me watching his back. I am wondering what has caught his attention, what he has found there, when a powerful jet breaks the water surface. In the midst of the tumult, Harry stares straight ahead as if there's something of interest on the wall in front of him.

130

We crawl further to the right and find another two doors, both locked. Almost on the opposite side, more or less where the entrance is in the basement, we come upon a door with a bare corridor behind it, tiled in functional white. My elbows and knees are sore and, without agreeing anything between us, we stand up and shuffle through the corridor with our backs against the wall. Now and then Harry flicks on the torch. The corridor is narrow and has a low ceiling, more a tunnel really. Three corners later, behind a heavy door with a hydraulic closer, we find the stairs, no wider than an ordinary staircase in an ordinary house.

Harry sits down on the bottom step and shines the torch higher. It reveals little: after a narrow landing the stairs change direction. Strands of dust hang from the bottom of the next flight, swinging slowly and weightlessly like unknown sea creatures in the depths of the ocean, illuminated for the first time.

We let the images sink in until we are familiar with every detail. In Harry's face, lit by the glow of the torch, I recognize my own horror at climbing the stairs and leaving the safety of the ground floor behind us. One well-chosen word, spoken in the right tone of voice, could change everything. I don't know where to find them, but that word and tone of voice do exist. Harry's sitting down betrayed their existence.

Maybe Harry will suddenly say the word, thirty or fifteen or five seconds from now, without suspecting my thoughts. The way he didn't suspect I had been thinking about Arthur when he suddenly said his name. Nothing special.

Afterwards Harry will stand up. Without making any fuss, we'll simply turn back. Giving each other a comradely pat on the shoulder or symbolically shaking hands before walking side by side down the long corridor to the lobby, which we cross calmly. This time we'll feast our eyes on it all. We'll take the towels from the toilet, the coat hangers, the perfumed toilet paper. We'll climb up one last time to fetch the wicker baskets and say goodbye, then pull the lift doors back until they meet in the middle, let the hatch bang shut and slide the table and soap barrels out onto the basement floor.

131

We've climbed four times sixteen steps without any sign of the first floor.

We carry on cautiously, making sure not to let the soles of our shoes slide on the steps. As soon as Harry's head reaches the level of the next landing, he stops and inspects it with the torch.

We keep climbing. There are neither doors nor windows on the landings. I've stopped counting. I am convinced that the stairs lead directly to the roof. Stairs for maintenance access. How else would they get to the machine room if the lifts broke down?

A little further up, the stairs come out on a small floor or spacious landing, the size of the garages in the basement. A lost space without any objects. No continuation of the stairs. We can't possibly be near the roof yet.

Harry slides the light slowly over the walls.

The door doesn't have a knob. On closer inspection we see the prints of dirty fingers where the knob would usually be. Hesitantly I press the spot with my index finger: the click of a magnetic lock. The fibreboard door swings a few centimetres towards us. Harry and I drop onto our left knees, out of the firing line, and aim, together with the torch, our Flocks at the crack.

Behind the fibreboard door, in a room not much larger than a shower cubicle, an ironing board is leaning against the wall, palm trees on its bleached and tattered cover.

A blue bucket is hanging from one of the legs.

It's so unexpected that the whole strikes me as some kind of greeting or secret message, set up here for us long ago.

132

Daylight. It is dim, the light of a cloudy afternoon that has reached here after detouring through rooms and around corners and down metres of hallway. But there is no doubt that it is natural light which, as dim as it is, demotes the torch to the level of a toy, a battery-operated gadget for projecting circles. Daylight comes first. The moment Harry pushes the door on the opposite side of the tiny room away from its magnet, there is daylight on our black leather shoes, on the scratchy carpet, on the plaster decorations on the hallway walls, on our hands, on our grey faces, in our ears: daylight everywhere. Its wholesome effect kicks in immediately.

133

Like the plaster monkeys on the wall, we're squatting. See no evil, hear no evil, speak no evil. The work of an amateur with no sense of proportion. We stick close to the ground.

The blue of our uniform looks different from downstairs, more frivolous.

In a small kitchen we sit on the floor with our backs to the cupboards and the barrels of our pistols up near our noses. At first sight, there's nobody. The stench rising from the pedal bin effortlessly overpowers the metallic smell of the Flock. A sliding door can be pulled shut to separate the kitchen from the living room. Through the legs of the table and the chairs, I see a shabby lounge suite, caramel coloured. The sofa bathes in the daylight pouring in through the window, which is uncurtained and covers almost the full length of the wall.

We stay sitting there for a long time. If someone has hidden themselves away, they must think we've gone again by now. But we don't hear anyone. Harry turns his head, his beard scraping and rustling over his collar. He looks me deep in the eyes, then nods.

Halfway into the living room the vast firmament is a dazzling grey. Solemnly we walk over to the window, taking slow considered steps, awed and anxious about the view the city below us will provide. On the long windowsill, close to the middle, is a round fishbowl. The evaporated water has left a filthy green coating three-quarters of the way up the glass.

134

I hear Harry speaking. He's saying something, not whispering. His words haven't got through to me yet. There's too much information to process in this hallucinatory chaos. The view is overwhelming and therefore meaningless: my eyes are no longer used to panoramas. It's the outskirts of a city, I recognize that much, but essentially see it as one big patch below me on the earth's crust, extending to the foot of this building. I close my eyes and give myself a mental pep talk, using my most soothing voice. I compose myself and open my eyes, trying not to see everything at once, concentrating my vision as if looking through a straw. Two, three buildings. I see their walls, their shape; they're still standing. Buildings with windows and roofs. Roofs with cupolas, chimneys, tiles, strips of tar and zinc. I expand my field of vision, unable to confine it any longer, and again my eyes skip from one spot to the next. I can't detect any destruction, just buildings with windows and roofs. Here and there, the first green of spring emerging in the grey stone mass. I look at the horizon, where there's nothing special to see, where the countryside begins. The grey clouds covering the city contain rain, not soot or ash or dust. I look at a window closer by, as if I've only just remembered the people who must have inhabited this city, with the buildings as proof. I check all of the chimneys one after the other, searching for a wisp of smoke or steam. I search for movement. The pattern of the road network. I search for moving cars, intersections. We're up high, but not high enough to see over the roofs and into the streets. The windows again. The back of a T.V. A half-drawn curtain. The corner of a wardrobe. Toadstools with white dots on the glass of the window.

135

The remnants are lying on the bottom of the bowl, a shrivelled sack of pale yellow scales. The goldfish died of suffocation or starvation or both, the only visible victim of the situation outside. Its dark eye has subsided and is staring inwards, as if desperate to turn away from what it saw from the windowsill.

Was the goldfish forgotten because it was everybody's and nobody's? Or did the difficulties prevent the owner from returning to the apartment, leaving them with a sickly sense of impotence every time they ate or drank?

This is just the first floor, Harry tells me. I might not believe it, but it's true. None of our wealthy residents would have bought a first-floor apartment if the windows only provided a view of the windows of a neighbouring building. That's why the first floor is much higher than usual. He says we're in the wrong place for a good view of the city.

In the kitchen he opens the cupboards. It's a kitchen that was rarely, if ever, used for cooking. The apartment's real kitchen, the large one where all of the meals were prepared, can't be far away either. This one was for talking, sitting around, eating sandwiches or warming up leftovers. Two cupboards are filled with glasses, mugs and plates. Harry finds a canister of fish food and the instructions for a coffee machine that's nowhere in sight. He picks out two sets of cutlery from the cutlery drawer and puts them in the inside pocket of his jacket, as if it's not food that's been in short supply, but knives, forks and spoons. In the fridge, a tin rolls around in the bottom of the vegetable drawer.

"Drink up," Harry says. "You can use it."

He hands me a garish fortifying drink.

Why can I use it more than him?

"We'll share," I say assertively.

"Of course we'll share," Harry says. "Hurry up."

I sit down on the armrest of the sofa and guzzle frenzied fizz that tingles in my nose and eyes; I don't taste a thing. While Harry's drinking, I notice a magazine in a wooden rack between the sofa and the window. It dates from before the exodus. On the front page a celebrity turns her bloodshot eyes away from the camera. On her arm, a man who does look into the lens, angry and desperate. They are hurriedly leaving a building. The caption under the photo: "Why won't they let us be happy?"

"Check out those boobs," Harry says.

I open the magazine; the paper has turned stiff. In her preface, the editor reviews the contents. Not the slightest insinuation of a political or social issue. I leaf on, diagonally scanning the blocks of text: births, marriages, illness, deaths, the normal entertainment. I study the cartoon, which goes on about the couple on the cover and their impossible happiness. They're featured in their underwear, the woman bare-breasted. Her nipples, indented around the edges as if they're flowers, reach out to the warmth of the spotlights. I study the crossword, the ads. I leaf back, looking at all of the faces, captions, the questions in bold face. One

190

catches my eye. A man in his fifties with an old-fashioned tapered moustache, a singer or a soap star, posing on a motorbike in front of a villa, is asked if things are different now, given recent events, from how they were before. As far as that's concerned, the man replies, a celebrity like him is no different from ordinary people and equal before the law. Plus he has to set an example.

136

In the hall, behind another storeroom with two doors, this time with coats on hooks, we find more stairs. The height difference to the second floor is considerably less. We take the time to climb in silence, on our guard. On the fourth floor we come out on a landing that extends for a good fifty metres and leads to the continuation of the stairs. Harry says, with one foot on the new stairs, that it doesn't make any bloody sense. He asks if it makes sense to me. I get the strong impression, I say, that originally they didn't plan for stairs. When they were forced to include them after all, this is what they came up with, squeezing them in left and right. I tell him I don't know either. On the next floor up, the stairs go down again at the end of the landing. It's unclear how many steps. Harry doesn't trust it and hugs the wall, lowering his feet slowly as if the steps are made of rotten wood, high above a ravine.

137

We've counted properly and haven't let the stairs' antics get to us. Or is it just an unlikely coincidence? When we enter the apartment, separated from the stairwell by an elongated room tiled in the same white as the narrow hall on the ground floor, we're standing almost next to the service lift, another neutral environment in plain grey. Mounted on the wall opposite the lift is an elegant brushed-aluminium plate in which a 2 and a 9 have been stamped; the indicator in the frame reads -1. I whisper that the stairs wind their way around the building and have brought us back to the lifts after all, but Harry isn't listening to my explanations. He aims the torch at the wall between us and the residents' and visitors' lifts. He presses his ear against it; I wait, holding my breath.

No daylight in these halls. Night has fallen, we've been going almost four hours. These staff quarters clearly have a different layout from the ones on the first floor. There is no kitchen adjoining the living room. A table and chairs, no lounge suite. The chairs are arranged willy-nilly, as if the people left in a hurry. Harry and I sit on the floor and try to relax. The torch shines across the floor, casting long shadows behind crumbs and dirt and balls of fluff.

The square window with a view of the starless sky: suddenly I think of the city below us and creep over to the window with Harry lighting my way. He asks what I'm doing and follows me.

Big dark patches, businesses, department stores or housing blocks, demarcated by street lights. I can't see any cars driving in the streets close by. Lit windows are few; it could be five a.m. I search for T.V. sets, but don't find any. I do spot a traffic light. Just the top of it, the red light, nothing of the intersection itself. When I fix my eyes on it, this is the only movement I detect in my entire field of vision: the red light flicking on and turning off again. And the varying intensity of the full moon behind the thin layer of cloud.

138

We come upon swing doors with small porthole windows and know that we needn't look any further. Where else would they use swing doors except between the service section and the luxury apartment? The sides of the doors are lined with silky-soft brushes. The torch smears a bluish-black gleam over the velvet that covers the backs of the doors from top to bottom, with the exception of one gold-coloured circle, split neatly into two halves down the middle: Plexiglas for pushing the doors open. It's dark behind the portholes.

Harry and I ball ourselves up against the wall. How are we going to do this? Without posing the question, we both search anxiously for an answer. It goes without saying that the resident will have a gun at his disposal. Even a bullet from an elegant lady's pistol can be fatal. He's lying in bed, unable to sleep from worry, and hears thumping in the apartment. It's not unexpected. He's always known that the war would one day reach his floor.

Then someone calls him, and someone else, over and over again, so reticent and suspicious that he decides not to deviate from his decision. They claim to be guards. Michel and Harry from the basement. The names of the poor buggers whose throats they just cut, their last words their own Christian names. He'll stay still, he'll stay lying in his bed in the darkness, something no intruder who announces himself would ever suspect. He'll take his time to aim properly and, even if he's noticed, with his arms on the duvet folded back in front of him and thick pillows behind his back and shoulders, their astonishment will give him a good two-shot advantage.

Harry's right though when he whispers that we can't just burst in on him. If we don't say anything and try to take him by surprise, it could turn out very badly. We have to avoid getting into a scuffle. We have to identify ourselves and hope that the resident keeps a cool head.

139

The wainscoting in the high-ceilinged hall behind the swing doors makes us feel like we have entered a country manor. There are no lights on anywhere. After so many hours of watchfulness, it's a real effort to raise our voices. Harry takes the lead, announcing our presence, giving the name of the organization. As long as he's shouting, I'm deaf to anything else and someone could come up behind me and shoot Harry straight through my head. I call out now and then too. We're two frightened children trying to chase away the woodland spirits by making lots of noise.

Everything in the apartment looks big and heavy. Bigger than usual, no doubt of that, but so oversized that even the enormous living room doesn't bring them back to normal proportions. Perhaps because of the shadows. A serrated bar to hang a kettle off extends out of the brick fireplace. It's hard to believe we're in a city, twenty-nine floors up and not in the English countryside. We walk from a living room to a salon, through a book-filled library to another study. In the sleeping quarters we lower the volume of our calls. The bedrooms have thick carpets and romantic wallpaper, four-poster beds with heavy, turned woodwork. All six of them are empty. No signs of life anywhere. Harry whispers that he's hiding from us. He warns the resident that we'll have to search for him and explains that we've come to get him because it's all become much too dangerous for him to stay here alone. I add that we can't possibly leave without him. I notice that my tone of voice is lower, less commanding. We stand there motionless, giving our words time to sink in.

140

Far from the sleeping quarters, in a billiard room with four doors, we stop for a moment. The balls are arranged neatly on the table. On the way here, Harry and I called out loudly once more, insisting that the resident show himself, to no avail.

"I know he's in the apartment," Harry whispers confidently. He means, I'm quite capable of counting to forty, but that wasn't even necessary, because only thirty-nine residents left the building. He suggests we lie low for a while with the torch off. The man's trembling in a wardrobe somewhere. If we keep quiet long enough, he'll get curious and come out of his hole and then we'll find him soon enough.

I don't ask why there aren't any lights on anywhere. Has the resident been living without electricity? Did he hear us coming? Did he see us, our caps, our uniforms? Did he catch a glimpse of our emaciated, bearded faces as we waved the torch around and take us for two murderers from the back streets of the city?

We leave the billiard room and keep watch in one of the halls. For about twenty silent minutes we stand in the dark with our Flocks in our hands. Then Harry comes closer and whispers slowly, "Maybe something's happened. To the resident."

I hear a cow moo. She'd already started while Harry was talking. I hear the last half of an angry outburst, although the sound hardly differs from the silence. Can I hear a cow here, behind eight centimetres of glass, behind walls that are thicker than the length of Arthur's arms? Wouldn't the cow have to be standing right in front of the building? There it is again: agitated, a quick succession of short, powerful, identical moos. More bellow than moo. I see the head and neck stretched out, eyes bulging, breath steaming out of her warm lungs. The sound in the night has a piercing loneliness. Is it because we're up so high? Is there a direct line from the apartment to the field the animal is standing in, without anything in between? Has the sound been sucked in through a ventilation shaft and funnelled into the apartment?

I'd like to ask Harry if he's heard it, but I don't want to erase the bellowing with my own voice. I feel that my silence draws his attention to the sound. A cow. A living animal not far from here, that hasn't been eaten.

141

"Harry?" More than really whispering, I mouth his name. We were making our way up the hall when I heard something behind us and stopped: a vague murmur, suddenly drowned out by the rustling of Harry's uniform, quite far away from me, short but remarkably loud, as if he's done something like quickly rub his arm over his torso or raise a knee, just once. I turn in that direction and mouth his name again, panting it out a little louder. I feel in the pitch darkness with one long arm. He's no longer there. "Harry?" More than five seconds pass. As if someone is holding me underwater and I've used up all of the air in my lungs. I can't stay here. I grope my way back to where I think I last heard Harry. "Harry?" I press the button on my watch three times, pointing the light in different directions, because I'm standing in a doorway and a metre further, the pale gleam of the dial shows another hall at right angles to the one I'm in. I wait, listen, stare. I think of Harry who could be standing still and waiting somewhere close at hand. I speak to him in my thoughts, beaming out my concentration like an antenna. I shuffle around the corner, to the right, searching for doorways, rooms. "Harry?" I squat; my mouth is dry, my tongue swollen. Why doesn't he flick the torch on just once? Has something happened to him? Has he discovered something? I crawl on all fours back to the spot where I lost him twenty minutes ago. I curse myself. Perhaps we've lost each other because I didn't stay put. Why didn't I stay where I was? I try to summon up the sound of his uniform again, the movement that made it rustle. Has someone overpowered him? "Harry?"

142

The dawn comes as deliverance. When the black has changed to the deepest blue and the sky is unmistakably growing lighter, Harry disappears from my thoughts for a moment. I look up from the floor at the large window as if it's a cinema screen. It's a spectacle I haven't seen for a long time and after a tense night it moves me to tears: the comforting proof that at least these certainties – the earth revolving on its axis, the existence of the sun – have remained unaffected.

143

I spend the whole day hiding behind a tall armchair. I have ripped open two cushions, with embroidered hunting dogs and flying ducks, and slowly saturated the pale balls of cotton wool with my dark-yellow pee. I haven't been able to make out any other sounds. No bellowing, no rustling garments, no man climbing out of a wardrobe. Lying down, I've stared out over the floorboards.

Either Harry's dead or Harry thinks I'm dead.

And where is the last resident? Is he the one who got Harry? Is Harry's lifeless body now lying somewhere on oak floorboards just like these, stiffening in position?

The chance of Harry walking in, saying my name and then laughing as he asks what I'm doing hiding behind a chair, that chance only existed briefly at daybreak. Still, I try to banish all other thoughts. I wait for his footsteps, the tap of his trouser hem against the smooth shoe. I wait where I am.

144

Late in the afternoon my tummy rumbles. It must be audible in the adjoining room and the two halls that lead into this one, maybe even further. I grab my ankles and curl my body up tight, tensing my abdominal muscles to drive out the growling.

Later cooling sweat sends shivers down my spine.

Towards dusk, the confined space behind the armchair is a prison and the urge to stand up grows too strong.

My perspective changes dramatically.

I fit the interior.

Otherwise nothing else happens. The air in the room stays still. I could just as well have spent the whole day standing like I am now, with my hands on the back of the armchair. I could have sat in the chair all day. Nobody would have noticed.

145

I can only see high-rise. It undoubtedly adds to the charm of the apartments, their looking out over the other tall buildings in the centre of town. Especially now, at the start of the evening, the view is irresistible. The streets remain hidden, as if intentionally. Again there are electric lights, but again there is an absence of any movement that suggests the presence of humans. In the clear sky I can't see any dissipating vapour trails from passenger jets. Only a purplish dot, far away, that soon disappears between invisible layers of air. The sky is empty and endless. The sunset casts a spell on me. For more than fifteen minutes, I don't look over my shoulder; until the sun has gone down, I am immortal. Maybe Harry and I were profoundly mistaken and right now parents are popping out to the supermarket to buy some meat, a carton of milk, some butter. A beautiful blonde in a black dress rearranges the wine glasses on Table 18, while the first customers enter the restaurant, waiting politely in the entrance hall for her to come over. In a vending machine in the train station concourse a chocolate bar with peanuts slides towards the edge of the abyss.

146

I creep around in the dark. The resident can't possibly still be hiding in a wardrobe. Harry has gone looking for him, just like me. The resident comes first. If I find the resident, I'll probably find Harry too. We just lost each other in the dark. I should have stayed where I was, but I didn't. Harry had his Flock in his hand, his finger on the trigger. Even taken by complete surprise, even if a piano wire had been tossed over his head and pulled tight around his throat by a burly man, he would have still got off a shot. That didn't happen either. Since he, just like me, doesn't know what's going on with the resident, he's keeping a low profile. On the other side of the manor, he's sweeping the dust and dirt away from the edges of the rooms, just as I'm doing in this wing. One thousand square metres. I turn onto my back, carefully pull my shirtsleeves away from my bleeding elbows and make a small calculation. It seems ridiculous to me: one thousand square metres, that's forty metres by twenty-five! The apartments are definitely larger. Whoever claimed they were a thousand square metres? I can't remember. Was it Arthur? Was he using "a thousand" as a figure of speech to show how big they are? As a symbol of the residents' extraordinary wealth? Their insatiable extravagance?

147

I lay the Flock on my stomach, then open and close my hand to avoid cramp. I am lying motionless on the floor, my arms alongside my body as if I'm waiting for the doctor and have already lain down on the bed. Has Harry started adding it up now as well? Does the apartment seem larger to me because I've never been here before and have no overview? Familiarity makes everything smaller. What's more, I'm looking at it all in moonlight from floor level. The walls are two storeys high.

On display in the middle of the room is a large design object with steel cables and several chromed tubes. A piece of fitness equipment. I can't think of any other purpose. Two serious men look down on the device disapprovingly from their dark portraits on the wainscoting.

I mustn't fall asleep. Despite everything, I feel as if I could fall asleep effortlessly, with a brief, blissful awareness of it happening, me disappearing into myself. I scratch my beard, stick a finger in one ear and jiggle it as quickly as I can. The pleasure spreads over my skull, opening my mouth and refreshing me. After the noise has left my head and I can hear the silence again, I press in the safety catch and strip the Flock: slide, barrel with chamber, recoil spring guide. I keep my eyes on the dark-swathed ceiling. Twice I overcome the resistance of the trigger: two clear clicks of the hammer and firing pin. For a few seconds, the parts are spread out on my stomach. Nobody notices it. Nobody seizes the opportunity. Then I click and slide everything back into place and it is as if the pistol, which I haven't really cleaned, is brand new again and extremely reliable.

148

Perhaps I'm leaving a trail. When it gets light, my trail will be as visible as the slime of a snail that has been dragging itself around all night. Although I am certain it's the same apartment, I don't encounter anything that fits in with last night's journey with Harry. The swing doors are unfindable, but the kitchen isn't necessarily close to the swing doors; nothing here can be taken for granted. Everything looks the same, but I don't recognize anything. I might as well be equipped with a faulty compass and surrounded by a swarm of mosquitoes in the barren landscape of the far North. I wouldn't feel any more lost than here between the tapestries, candelabras and carved chests, faint with hunger.

149

A step. I feel another one higher up. I light the way with my watch. I'm far from any windows, in the heart of the apartment, somewhere in a small room. Narrow, wooden steps like the kind that lead up to a mezzanine or an attic. It's close to morning, maybe the other rooms are already getting lighter. I haven't heard a thing all night. The resident isn't on this floor. He's either dead or alive. If he's alive, he must have fled out of fear, upwards perhaps, to a higher floor. He expected the danger to come from below, merciless, like water rising in a flood. I creep up. The staircase is short, two or three metres, that's all. I expect an intermediate level, a workroom, studio or loft, but my hand doesn't feel the oak floorboards I'm used to. I feel the chill of stone. I enter a room that amplifies every noise I make. It reminds me of the landings Harry and I crossed earlier. Some distance further along a new staircase begins, made of stone like the stairs between floors. Have I found my way back into the stairwell near the swing doors? Or is there more than one set of stairs? Are the apartments not only larger than a thousand square metres, but with layouts and dimensions that vary completely from one to the next?

150

Slinking is ridiculous and pointless. Except for the white marble columns, a double row of three, the imposing hall is virtually bare: every corner is exposed. I am alone. I stand up. I stand on two feet like a man. Is this a mosque? I see a vision of grey prayer rooms hidden behind faded warehouse gates, with cables and pipes visible on the walls, with low, false ceilings. But this makes me think of Mohammedan temples on the banks of the Euphrates. Every square centimetre is covered with tiles, together representing garlands of flowers, olive branches and symmetrical vines, blue, yellow, reddish brown, green, in numbers and patterns that make my head spin. I can hardly bear it. So much profusion is overwhelming. I concentrate on the low benches against the walls: they're continuous, they pass under the keyhole-shaped windows and trace the perimeter of the hall like overgrown skirting boards. On the very far side there is a small interior balcony. But no carpets, not even a doormat. In the middle, the floor is a kaleidoscopic compass rose, a mosaic of the most colourful kinds of stone beneath a gold-leaf-covered chandelier as big as a treetop.

There, in the centre, I also see myself. I see my uniform, stained and sagging. My cheap black shoes, my ruffian's face. I feel like a desecrator. I'm still wearing my cap on my head.

151

I sweep the aluminium plate with the dim light of my watch. Two threes. I'm on the thirty-third floor. I repeat the sentence in my head, as if putting a seal on a certificate. With my back against the wall, I slide down onto the floor.

The stairs connecting the floors to each other are meant for domestic staff only. They share a single employer, after all. The residents have purchased the service, but that doesn't make them their bosses. That's why the staff can disappear into *trompe l'oeils* like Regency period servants and slip down secret corridors on their way to another floor, climbing wooden attic stairs to get there if necessary.

I stare at the red light in the frame for so long that the −1 becomes meaningless and it takes me a while to realize that it's suddenly gone off. I keep looking at exactly the same spot. When I blink, I see it appear again as a vague glow. The after-image is displaced by a new light. It's the same red, at most a little brighter, and now shaped like a zero.

For a short period I am convinced that I am controlling the light with my brain, through my gaze. I think of 1, I think of 2, and, *look*, the numbers light up before my eyes. It's only at 4 that I hear something, a weak, subterranean rumbling, and only at 5, a handful of seconds after the disappearance of −1, that it hits me like a bucket of ice water: the service lift is moving.

Breathlessly I follow the numbers, trying to avert them. 20 is a turning point. The moment I see that I haven't succeeded in stopping it at 20, I realize in the darkness preceding 21 that the lift is headed for this floor, 33, and me.

152

I'm sitting in front of the lift with both hands clamped around the grip of the Flock. My relaxed arms are resting on my raised knees. I'd hit the bullseye at fifty metres.

I concentrate on the sliding doors, no longer looking at the red numbers.

A sucking sound as it brakes, starting high and getting lower. The familiar signal.

After a moment's hesitation, the doors slide swiftly open.

I see the table in a sea of light.

It is as if the lift is presenting me with the table.

The hatch through which Harry and I climbed up onto the roof of the cabin is still open.

The door stays open longer than usual.

I start to get a nasty feeling that something is expected of me. The lift has come to visit me of its own accord to present me with the table. It's my turn.

Again I check the corners of the cabin. The table can't hide anyone, therefore there is no-one in the lift. Just the table.

Then I catch sight of the control panel. Because I'm sitting on the ground, I notice a slightly larger button at the bottom, separate from the long row like the dot of an exclamation mark. There is a picture of a red telephone on it. Next to it, thin vertical stripes indicate a built-in speaker.

What would happen if I pressed that button? Would I get someone on the line: a call centre, a young woman asking how she can help me?

But when I enquire about the situation outside, she skilfully avoids answering. She repeats her question, asking how she can help me, if there's a problem with the lift. She quotes the address. She looks at the dot in the area shaded red on the map on her wall. She has been selected for her high tolerance. They've taught her techniques; it's impossible to throw her off balance. I can curse, rant and rave, the woman's voice coming out of the speaker will sound just as cheerful and she will give away just as little. They have impressed upon her that someone can be listening in. Sometimes. She doesn't know when. She has to placate the client; that's her number one priority. She has to give the client the impression that help will be arriving shortly. That is the only service she is able to provide: lying. She has bunched her hair together in a ponytail on the top of her head. The ends curl in. In the toilet she dabs the corners of her eyes with a tissue, controlled and systematically, until the tears stop coming. She introduces herself as Julie, but her name is Isabelle.

I get up and walk slowly to the light-filled cabin. Just to hear Isabelle's voice! I am willing to play the game. I won't make her lies any more difficult and I'll ask her if she can send someone soon to fix the lift.

Close to the cabin I hear a double click and all at once the two doors slide towards the middle. I pull my arm back and stiffen. For a couple of seconds I have a clear view of the planks that make up the tabletop, with a lengthwise strip of unstained grey wood, a rough silhouette of a body.

The lift stays where it is.

Has Harry sent the lift because he's back in the basement with the last resident safe in the storeroom? But how would he know I'm on 33? It must have been me, groping around in the dark. I must have pushed the button to call the lift myself. In the basement the doors resumed their struggle with the barrels of liquid soap and finally won.

I make myself scarce. My position is known.

153

I open my eyes. The sunlight is as sharp as broken glass, slashing my brains. Within seconds, pain has filled my head. I have slept. I'm lying on my back on a parquet floor and feel very precisely the points where my skeleton has been resting on the wood for hours. If I want to get up I'll have to move, but what should I try to move first?

I raise my arm uncertainly, as if I'm pushing my limits with an overly ambitious weight. The cumbersome thing waves over my chest and stops ten centimetres in front of my face. I read 11:17 on my watch. With a thud, the arm falls on my hip and rolls to the floor. Sleeping has exhausted me.

The radiator near my shoulder has thick, decorative elements. Descending from the high ceiling are several angular chalices, orange glass in black frames, finished with fringed trim; they hang down as low as the standard lamps are high. In a single, exhausting movement, I hoist myself up onto all fours. I let my head hang for a moment, until the dizziness from my low blood pressure passes. Then I move to a squat, laying the Flock aside, picking up my cap and arranging it on my head at the prescribed angle. Dark blocks of wood are set into the parquet, forming dotted lines across the breadth of the room.

I lean heavily on a low, narrow table against the back of a long sofa. I see my hand lying next to a dish, an even dark blue with a gold rim, containing brooches, rings, bracelets and pearl necklaces, as if they were candy or pieces of fruit to pop in your mouth casually in the course of the day.

154

I see the newspaper from a distance. It's lying next to an antique crystal bowl on a gleaming cherry sideboard. It is folded neatly, but yellowed and wrinkled, as if it has been removed sopping wet from a letterbox and never read. That last bit is highly likely: the dateline is the day before the great exodus.

Like a dog snatching a piece of sausage, I grab the newspaper and throw myself on the floor. My heart is pounding, my hands trembling. I expect a headline that will explain everything in one glance, five or six words that will reveal all the things Harry and I could only guess at in the basement. On the upper left, in a typeface from the top of the case, I immediately strike gold: "Army ignores bills". While running my eyes over the lead, "Defence launches internal investigation", I try to reconcile this news with the events that followed it, but that proves difficult. I read the sentence in the middle of the article that has been printed in slightly larger, red letters to attract the readers' attention. "The water in the barracks was almost cut off because of the unpaid 10,000 euro bill." I read the words again, perplexed. Then the start of the article, which repeats everything I've read so far. Negligence in a few barracks, after which the ministry of defence launched an internal investigation.

Unpaid bills? Could unpaid bills have been the germ of a conflict that, for reasons unknown to me, led to the city emptying shortly afterwards?

At the bottom of the page is another article about the army: the three large cities in the south of the province have called in the army to assist with rubbish collection until an agreement has been reached with the unions. On page three, again: "Army helicopter hits power line". The emergency landing turns out to have been successful, the crew unharmed: seven soldiers thank and praise the pilot.

I race through every headline in the paper. Not one sounds like something big is about to happen. But . . . if the catastrophe had emerged a few days beforehand, would the newspaper have been left unread on a sideboard?

In the culture section I discover a photo of the celebrity I saw

210

red-eyed and with a man on her arm in the magazine on the first floor. She's beaming happily. Her dazzling evening dress only just covers the secret of her success. The man is not in the picture. A mourning band has been superimposed on the upper left-hand corner of the photo because the woman jumped out of a window of the Hilton Hotel the day before. The awning over the entrance did a good job of breaking her fall but the solid radiator grill of the parked limousine, a Hummer, still crushed her skull. Her death is considered in detail over four pages. Some people point the finger of accusation at the popular media. Others are sure she was pushed.

155

I reread the newspaper from front to back, concentrating on every sentence. Somewhere among the events that took place two days before the exodus and were reported on its eve, there must be some indication of the spark, the flicker that seemed innocent at first but soon caused an inferno. I have the solution in my hands. But the longer I read and search, the more it seems as if the words and sentences are wilfully barricading the path to an explanation. It's as if my view of the news is being blocked by a smokescreen of banality raised by a select group of writers acting on the orders of the security services. A practice that virtually everyone knew about, but no-one rebelled against. Perhaps out of fear of reprisals or social isolation. Perhaps from naked indifference. Maybe everyone knew what was going on, but no-one wanted to be reminded of it. That could explain the disproportionate attention for this celebrity and the account of her suicide. A story, what's more, that fell into the writers' laps ready-made.

I close the paper and look across the parquet and between the furniture at the doors. Then I try to forget all the thoughts I've had so far. In my hands I am holding a completely ordinary newspaper, which contains facts about things that really happened, covered by an independent editorial staff because of their newsworthiness. These facts may cast a light on the events of the following day. I take a deep breath and begin reading at the top of the page on the left, about unpaid army bills.

156

The fridge looks as massive as a monolith. The corners and edges are rounded off, even the door is slightly convex. The brand is shining in small signature letters on a stripe on the door. Everything in the kitchen interior is matching and wearisome because of the excess of bright colours.

With one hand on the handle, I feel like I am breaking an unwritten law. As if it is only after opening the fridge and revealing what they eat that I will have fundamentally trespassed in the residents' intimate sphere; me, a guard who is meant to protect the residents from such infringements.

I look at my hand, at the determined white of my knuckles, the precursor to a release of the energy building up in my shoulder.

What am I doing here?

This fridge, this kitchen, these colours: they were never meant for me.

What, after all, did the guard tell us that gave us the right to leave the basement and enter the clients' apartments?

The organization hasn't given us a mandate. It's true that Harry and I are searching for the last resident to move him to safety, but no-one ordered us to do so. We are still only authorized for the basement of this building.

157

I smell her perfume, the herbs and spices, thyme, rosemary, nutmeg, I smell the simmering, the sizzling beef, fresh soup vegetables chopped up on the board, onion and bay leaves, boiled marrowbones and steaming meat stock, chicken pastries in the oven, a joint of venison braising in port, spoonful by spoonful, the lid in the air while the steam is sucked up by the extractor fan, billowing up around the sides of the hood, condensed steam dripping from the lid and dancing on a glowing hotplate. She wipes her red hands on her apron, which pinches her waist like a string tied round a joint of rolled meat and covers the skirts that surround her thighs like layers of puff pastry. Her fingertips scored with dozens of nicks that always contain the taste of food.

158

She doesn't tug on the handle, but opens the door with a twist of her wrist. She is shorter than me, about ten centimetres, and it's a big fridge; she doesn't need to bend to get a good view of its contents. If she wants something from the back of the top shelf, she has to stretch and go up on her toes, just slightly, as if giving her weight a nudge, momentarily bouncing it up into the air, just long enough for her plump hand to grab what she needs.

I'm sitting at the table with my hands on my thighs to avoid seeming pushy. I'll let Claudia give me whatever she likes. She slides sideways along the worktop with her stomach resting on the front edge, as if she's attached to it. This is her kitchen. At least, the kitchen she works in daily. Her kitchen would look different, more rural, chunkier, with a water pump and a big sink.

I see the way her lower legs taper down to ankle folds. There's something glittering on the left, a gold chain, as thin as if it's for the wrist of a newborn; resting on the top of her bare foot. Surprisingly, she is also wearing heels. They are low, wide at the top but descending almost to a point: timeless women's shoes, bordering on seductive.

Soon she will turn around. I'll look her in the face, which, as always, will be beautifully made up. Her eyes hardly need any colour. The edges of her eyelids, her eyebrows and lashes are naturally coal-black. Bending over the table, she will lay spotless cutlery to the left and right of an absent plate.

159

In the salon, she fluffs up the cushions. She unties my laces and cautiously removes my shoes, as if suspecting pain. I'm ashamed of the stench, but Claudia is discreet, she doesn't let it show. She lifts my legs up onto the sofa and sits down across from me, beneath a collection of handbags with solid, upright handles, ascending towards the ceiling on five columns of glass shelves. When she crosses her legs, her shoe slips off her heel and dangles from her toes. Dreamily, she looks out of the window at the clouds, humming. My gaze wanders to a black patent-leather handbag in the middle of the top row; it is shaped like a shell. Without looking at me, Claudia says it would be better if I shut my eyes for a moment.

160

We've secluded ourselves. We've locked doors to make a small home inside the enormous apartment. Claudia knows the ropes. She's worked here from the beginning. No-one except Claudia has ever operated the cooker, apart from Mrs Olano putting on the kettle at the crack of dawn to make some tea, or Mr Olano during a sleepless night, when his sick wife or someone or something has prevented a visit to Claudia and he's venting his anger with food. He has a right to much more than her hands, though he's never claimed it. Instead of Mrs Olano's stubble he wants to imagine pitch-black hair curling up exuberantly into her bum crack, and the beat of his pelvis sending waves up towards her waist, the tanned Mediterranean skin over her sploshing flesh; he wants to sink his teeth into it, really biting, tearing away a mouthful of this taunting abundance. It's his right; that is his deepest conviction. What would Claudia be without him, back in that impoverished country of hers with its pigs and peasants and suffocating traditions? He leans back on the cushions beneath the handbags, appraising his cigar while the smoke leaks out of the corner of his mouth. He wants me to tell him that. He says he's a reasonable man, that he's never demanded too much of life, always meant well by other people. I can ask anyone I like, no-one will speak badly of him. Someone who tries to please everyone must be self-centred: this insight comes to him at night when Mrs Olano's mouth has dropped open and she's blowing her sour breath at the moon. He delights in the realization and, for its duration, he, Carlos Olano, comes first and wants to bite, really bite, but not bones. He could devour Claudia's flesh, did I know that? But the long, dark passage to the staff quarters weakens his resolve. Standing at her bed, when she rolls over towards him, he only lays a warm hand on her high hip. He doesn't stroke her, he doesn't bite her, he doesn't push a finger in anywhere. None of that. Once the fire has been quenched by her hands, he might run the back of a little finger over her cheek, but then he's gone, because sooner rather than later contempt will flare up out of those smouldering ashes. He doesn't speak and in the daytime he never touches her. He keeps an amiable distance. It's only after her very best dishes that he sends the butler to fetch her so that he can compliment her while resting one hand on Mrs Olano's knee to reassure her, his beautiful, captivating wife, who grows melancholy from the desire in Claudia's eyes and realizes that she is attractive despite her size, not least of all to her Carlos, for whom she has borne two successors, two clever sons, two sweet boys, who are moved to tears by Mahler's Fifth, nestling their heads against her empty breasts; they will never leave her.

161

We listen and hear nothing. We're probably the only ones on the entire floor. It has grown dark. I've spent more than a full day here. Claudia says that everything is locked, that we'll definitely hear any intruders. Before sitting down, while bending her knees, she runs both hands over her bottom and the backs of her legs to smooth out her skirts. The room is moonlit: long, unrecognizable shadows hang from the handbags. Claudia tells me I have to think. First and foremost, a guard must think. Unlike most people, he can't just go at things. She says that always thinking is a guard's best way of protecting himself. That's where it starts. This is, above all else, his first task. If he only half protects himself, how can he protect a client? A guard who's let himself be eliminated is no guard, he's just a dead body, incapable of doing anything more than making his murderer stumble. He's worthless. Her upper body sags towards the armrest; pensively she rests her chin on her hand. She asks if I wouldn't mind washing just this once, the room reeks of my stench. Mrs Olano would show me the door, she loathes things that smell. No shortage of bathrooms. Even if the water's cut off, there will still be some left in the pipes, enough to run at least one bath.

162

She walks ahead of me, it's not far; it's already morning. A sarcophagus, that's what the block of granite most recalls. It's set into a deck of tropical hardwood in the middle of a room. A tub has been carved from the block, as rectangular as the stone itself. No taps anywhere. After Claudia presses the matt silver button, the water wells up quickly, then abruptly falls still, except for some quiet murmuring. She closes the glass door, which has no lock; the glass is only transparent at the top and bottom. She tells me I have to take off my uniform and removes my cap. My Flock moves from one hand to the other, back and forth, until I'm standing on the deck undressed. My stench is more pungent. Claudia looks me over from head to toe. After a while of not saying or doing anything, she touches my abdomen. She comes closer and joins me in looking down at her hand on my white belly, which is almost completely motionless. I feel her other hand on my backside. She whispers that it's a test. She means Harry. He wants to see how far I'll go. Whether I'll freeze up with fear or be resolute and carry on. If I can find the resident by myself and bring him back to the basement. She says that Harry took off deliberately. As a test.

163

My clothes are lying in a heap at my feet. I see the dirt between my toes and under my long nails. I have to pick up my clothes. My jacket needs hanging up, my trousers need folding. Claudia soothes me. She'll do it in a minute. Now I just have to lie back in the bath. It will refresh me. I'll feel reborn, a new man. She's fetched clothes out of Mr Olano's wardrobe, we're the same size. Spotless clothes made of the finest fabrics. Smelling of dried flowers, they lie here next to a pile of towels waiting for me. But slowly my aversion to submerging myself in the dark water in the cold room grows insurmountable. Claudia says I have to relax. Look at the way I'm squeezing my pistol. Look at my eyes, there, in the mirror. Her hand descends over the curve of my buttocks, slipping between my legs, carefully enclosing what it meets on its way.

164

She says Harry didn't come back. Normally he would have returned to where we lost each other, just as I returned. He would have waited there for a sign of life. But he didn't. He didn't send any signals either, not with his watch and not with the torch, even though he couldn't have been very far away. Claudia is sitting on the edge of the bath, leaning straight-armed on the granite, her heavy breasts raised miraculously by her high shoulders. She is, for a woman of her size, small and tight. She keeps looking down. She whispers that she wants to see it. On her tummy. When she sees it, she'll come too.

165

The bath drains without a sound. To me, it seems as if the mass of water is a solid object slowly sliding into the base of the sarcophagus. Maybe the pipes contain enough water for another bath; it doesn't matter. I pull my uniform back on. My stinking doesn't matter, it is my own stench. I don't want to be reborn. My name is Michel, I'm a guard. Mr Olano's clothes don't suit me. Claudia does up my tie, she speaks hesitantly. She says that of course Harry doesn't want to go to the elite with someone he can't count on, someone who can't take care of himself. A partner he has to constantly watch over. You can't do that in the elite. He wants to be sure of things, which is understandable. Because the elite does its guarding much closer to the client. There is no room for mistakes or losing time or inattentiveness. A single incident can seriously compromise people's trust in the organization. And, as I know, everything depends on that trust. Without that trust, the organization has no authority, no power. Everything that has been built up by thousands of dedicated guards, over the whole world, could be undone by a single blunder. Claudia asks me if I understand. She brushes off the shoulders of my jacket, takes a step back and looks at me.

166

I don't really believe that, do I? She repeats her question. She's lying stretched out on the sofa under the handbags, her right leg raised indolently, she's touching herself. Her breasts have sunk into her armpits; nipples as dark as chocolate, as big as the palm of a hand. She is only wearing her shoes. Sometimes she gives little taps. One hand encloses, the other taps. Do I hear her? The twenty-ninth floor, she doesn't think so. No, she doesn't believe a word of it. Harry deliberately gave the wrong floor so that he could shake me off in the confusion and leave me in uncertainty. He thought it out far in advance, even before the decision to move the resident to the basement. He knows full well which floor the resident lives on. He had me barking up the wrong tree. He wants to know if I listened to him properly, if I learnt anything in those hundreds and hundreds of days, if I'm primed, ready when necessary, and that's usually when it's completely unexpected. Claudia squints up at my member just above her forehead. She presses the top of her head back in the cushions, raises her chin in the air and opens her mouth a little. The deep folds in her neck open up as smooth white lines. Little by little the taps turn to blows.

167

I ask her to stay in the kitchen. She's distracting me. I'd rather not hear her. She doesn't even need to raise her voice: she talks as if I'm sitting at the table with her in the kitchen and that's enough. I roll my forehead over the cold window like a stamp and look down on the fossilized city. She tells me I have every reason to be disillusioned. After all, what did I do to deserve this? Haven't I always done as he asked? Haven't I always shown my loyalty? How exactly does Harry expect me to fall short? Not once, Claudia says, has there been a serious incident. He and I were always one step ahead of trouble. What's more, I've spent hours and hours on guard duty alone, while Harry was asleep, when he, for all intents and purposes, wasn't there and the building was an undiminished forty luxury storeys high with defenceless rich people asleep on every one. She says he could have foreseen me asking myself these questions. He should have foreseen that I would look beyond first impressions and, sooner or later, guess his motives. Doesn't he realize that this man-oeuvre undermines everything we've achieved together? A test! What's he scared of?

168

—

I'm lying on the floor, rolled up in a ball, protecting myself.
I have been reduced to eyes, nose and ears. I have become my
face, a small animal living in the centre of a dark muggy cave.
Through a crack I see shiny leather shoes pointing in my direction. I move my head, my eyes rise up Mr Olano's evening dress
and skip over his bow tie to his face, spotlighted by the bright
sun. The gleam on his rigorously parted black hair. He blinks as
he tries to look into the cave. He pulls his left and right cuffs out
from under the sleeves of his dinner jacket and steps towards
me, kneeling, moving his mouth to the crack, breathing. I smell
peat, whisky, single-malt. Quietly he says that the competition
is murderous. He says that positions hardly ever come up. Who
wouldn't want to guard a roomy villa in body armour with
modern firearms? Patrolling magnificent gardens? Estates that are
guarded so well and in such numbers that the chance of an attack
is zero. A job for life. The twenty-ninth floor? No, he says. The
last resident doesn't live on 29 and Harry knew that all along.
No, he wasn't mistaken. Harry will escort the resident to the
basement and he'll do it alone. His achievement, his promotion.

169

Harry's dead. He's in a state of decomposition. It's as if I can't find anywhere in this immense building to put him down. I keep searching with his body slung over my shoulder; the reek of rotten potatoes. I try the stairs to a higher floor: head down, pulling his feet up and angling him across the steps, arms dramatically spreadeagled. A fatal fall. I leave him where he is for a moment. Yes, he's good there. When I come back, I don't like the look of those spread arms. I dislocate his shoulder and hide one arm under his torso. His shirt is bloodstained. He was dead before he hit the ground, he didn't feel any pain. I break his neck too, so that he's looking almost backwards. I take off a shoe and lay his cap a few metres away, blue satin up. I take him in from different perspectives. He doesn't look bad, but the location is slightly contrived. Maybe I should keep searching.

170

I can't worry about Harry anymore. I have to keep going. Until he shows up, I have to act like he doesn't exist. Claudia begs me to stay, hanging off my arm as I try to reach one of the locked doors. I drag her over the parquet. I feel compelled to intervene but even after a firm slap in the face – once the moment's astonishment has passed – she persists in holding on tightly to my trouser leg with both hands. I kick her. First lightly, as an announcement of intent, then harder, with the toe. I tell her I'll kick her full in the face, but that doesn't scare her. Suddenly I swing my leg away from her, as if kicking for goal; I hear her fingernails breaking.

I slam the door behind me, turning the key in the lock.

After a few seconds in the hall, I am struck by something familiar. At first I don't know what it is. Claudia leans against the other side of the door. She says it's walnut, a hint of fresh walnut, just fallen from the tree, with a hard green hull. She says he's looking for me. He fell behind. He had trouble finding all of the stairs and has only just reached this floor. She says he wants to play it safe, he doesn't want to squander the opportunity. He's planned it all. We lost each other and then a terrible accident happened. In the confusion I, Michel, died, fatally wounded by friendly fire. Harry is inconsolable, but he keeps his back straight, his chin up. You can't turn back the clock. This is what his trusty partner would have wanted: him dedicating himself completely to his new task.

171

Claudia and Mr Olano don't know Harry.

172

At the end of the hall I lie flat on my stomach. Am I imagining the smell I know so well? Am I imagining the smell because I hope it's a way to track down Harry without his noticing? And if I really can smell it, am I tracking him or is he lying in wait for me?

173

I creep along on my elbows, the scabs break open, the familiar pain flares in my bones. The day is coming to an end, twilight has laid claim to the halls and rooms. I combat my thirst with memories of drinking the bathwater, scooping it up out of the sarcophagus with my hands before it disappeared completely down the drain. I no longer think about how hungry I am. Hunger has become a part of me. Just as I have two arms, two legs and one head, I am hungry. I crawl through a portal and enter an atrium. White Roman busts in niches around me, radiating light. A draught drifts over the smooth floor and as I, breathing half through my mouth, pick up the smell I would recognize from thousands, I see a leg moving beside the central ornament, a foot, a black shoe slipping out of sight.

I don't even flinch, but still feel everything within me move. His name is on my lips, I'm about to softly blow life into it.

I manage to swallow it just in time.

174

Sometimes I hear Harry. While creeping along, he sometimes slides his shoes over the ground. It's not so much the sliding I hear, as the slight drag when the sole catches on a groove or a join in the floor.

175

He grew up on a farm in the north of the province with two brothers, Jim and Bob, guards like Harry. A pioneer family. With a war veteran dad to boot. I wrack my brains, but can't remember anything else. After all that time in the basement, this is what I actually know about Harry. After all that time washing his underwear with my bare hands.

176

Why bother reacting? What kind of answer should he have given to the announcement that it was, for instance, Wednesday? He could hardly object. I was the one who studied the calendar. Every morning he relied on my calculation. Maybe he listened, maybe he didn't. Maybe it didn't make any difference to him whether it was Wednesday or Thursday. And he was right; it didn't make any difference. But maybe, for a few minutes after my announcement, he did let the day of the week sink in. It's even possible that he kept a record of the days too. That his silence was a sign of assent. And that he would have corrected me, immediately, if I had made a mistake.

177

"You and me." He never said anything else, not once. He always said, "You and me." He always dreamt about the elite for both of us. Us, Harry and me, sitting in a garden a hundred times the size of the basement, out of harm's way in the countryside, enjoying a blue sky and eating juicy fruit. But nudging up the flush button in the toilet, the simplest of gestures, was too much for him, remembering to do that was beyond him, despite my repeated requests. Even though it was audible everywhere, enough to drive you mad, Harry stayed deaf to the whistling in the pipes. It was too much trouble for him, even for *his* Michel, with whom he, in the near future, would be promoted and by whose side he would spend many more years as a guard. Harry with his gruff, handsome, square face, always one step ahead, ordering me time and time again to think, to just think, mostly when what I thought was different from what he thought. Harry, who was tempted to waste ammunition on a fly.

178

How can he possibly not smell me? I've been following him for two hours now. I don't stink any less than him.

Does the pungency of walnut keep all other smells at bay?

I find it hard to believe he hasn't noticed anything. Sometimes I come very close to him, but not once does Harry stop for more than a few seconds to smell or listen.

Is he leading me somewhere?

Is he laughing to himself as his Flock comes down on the ground with yet another click?

179

It happens in a room filled with moonlight. In one continuous movement he goes from creeping to raising his pelvis, kneeling on his left knee, bringing his other leg forward under his body, putting his foot flat on the ground and pushing himself up with his hands on his thigh. I expect him to speak to me and half raise my body, as if I'm ashamed at having followed him in silence, my partner, him and me at the same post together for so long. I kneel behind him and off to one side in the doorway of the study Harry is ignoring: he looks out of the window at the city deep below us. I see the moon shining through his beard, casting a glow around his head, and him staying motionless as if he's not really looking, not really seeing anything, just staring into the night in a dream. His Flock hangs in his hand beside his upper leg, index finger curled around the trigger. Now that we're no longer hugging the ground, the distance between us is ridiculous, just four or five steps. I see him blink. Once. A man who is calm and has himself under control, the master of the situation, certain of what will come next. I look a fool here on my knees. Is that why he keeps looking out, to give me time to stand up? Is he allowing me time to compose myself after this shameless pursuit over several long hours, letting me assume a pose worthy of a guard? Or is he giving me time to think about how he has got me into this position: on my knees high in the building, trapped? Is he glowing on the inside, glorying in his advantage? Is he telling me through his silence, by making a show of not turning around: Look at yourself. Here I am, Harry, in the uniform that's made for me, cap perched on my head the way it's supposed to be, headed for the elite, where I belong, and there you are, Michel, been to university and all, down on your knees like a mangy, desperate beggar. I should finish you off like this, without turning around.

A flick of his eyelashes ripples the hush, after which I feel like I detect a different expression around his eye, as if he's on the point of breaking into a regretful smile or shaking his head disbelievingly. Is he thinking back on the past few days? Is he thinking back on them as if none of it happened to him, but to a different Harry, a Harry he doesn't know as well as he'd always thought? Is he surprised by that Harry? Is he thinking, how could I have been so completely wrong about someone? Or is Harry surprised at having stood on his feet for two full seconds without firing? Why wait any longer? Is there a word? Is there a word in the air in this study, ready to be spoken in the one correct tone, just a moment from now, a word that will defuse the situation, making space for a safe continuation, a second word that will introduce a third, a sentence that will end in a laugh? It must exist, if we both think hard enough. But maybe Harry's not thinking about anything in particular. Maybe he's looking out of the window and thinking I'm dead, and letting his thoughts wander wistfully through the past and the basement, set off by the moonlight, turning over distant memories and thinking: Back onto the ground in a minute, creeping along in search of the last resident, wherever he might live. But not just yet, not now. Harry doesn't move, it's like he's not there. In my position he wouldn't have a single doubt. How long did it take him to see through the guard? Could he have unmasked him any faster? All he needed was a porcelain cat, that one detail was enough. A porcelain cat! And I, Michel, actually saw the figurine before me, a white pussycat sitting on the shelf in his colleague's box. I saw the guard's empty shelf and his colleague's porcelain figurines, and Harry, he thought about it and smelt a rat. What would Harry make of it if *I* just disappeared, without so much as a signal, and didn't return to the spot where we lost sight of each other? Would I be allowed to flout an agreement? In the middle of an unauthorized operation? What would Harry do if I then allowed myself to be followed for hours and suddenly, without deigning to look at him, got up to stand there, unmoving, for three full seconds?

Harry doesn't move because he's waiting. He's waiting for me in the full light of the moon. He doesn't turn, knowing that the most innocent of movements will evoke other movements that will set off his instincts, instincts he has no control over, causing a chain reaction with an uncertain outcome. He's giving me time to think, briefly. He wants me to make the right decision, just as he would. I mustn't hesitate any longer. I must do what he has shown and taught me. I mustn't disappoint him. I want him to be proud of me. The old Harry. He's waiting for me. He's waiting out of love.

180

The study, which grew completely dark in the course of the night, regains its shape in the first timid daylight, its colour too. I'm sitting under the window holding Harry's hand on my thigh. He's looking in the other direction. He's listened to me, although

I've told him little. I explained to him that he was wrong, that Mr Toussaint's car is white too. A big white car. And that Mr Colet has nothing to do with the Olanos. I said, "Just believe me." And, "I heard it from Claudia. She's the one who baked the frangipane." At the word "frangipane" my mouth started to water. I repeated it a few times and drank my saliva. After a few times it stopped. Then I thought about the canister of fish food we found in a kitchen on the first floor, five or so metres from the goldfish. Just lying there in the kitchen cupboard. Printed cardboard with a shaker lid. I wondered what fish food could possibly be made of to make it inedible for humans. I considered the question seriously, but couldn't come up with anything and so decided, with a sense of victory, that the ingredients must all have organic origins. Nice and salty, to keep it from going off. I flicked the lid off with my fingernail and tipped the entire contents into my mouth, chewing on the dry flakes. Later, in the absolute silence, the sole of my foot started itching and I had to take my shoe off to scratch it. When I moved and let go of his hand, Harry seemed to softly squeeze my leg.

181

In my memory it was different: every time it seemed as if the Flock 28 was trying to take off, with the force of the recoil and the resistance of my arm making the pistol kick up. This felt more like a neurological short circuit, an electric charge suddenly cramping my whole arm, all the way up to my shoulder. It didn't sound like a shot. It was a dry, penetrating thump. I can still hear it, or better, feel it: an indentation on the eardrum like a wound on the roof of your mouth you can't stop running your tongue over. On exiting his head, the bullet tore away a piece of his cheekbone. In the daylight I see that the injury is clean, a hole I could stick my little finger into with white, broken bone around the edges. Below that hole, untouched skin and the start of his beard. Above it, his lifeless eye, an encapsulated eyeball. In the window the deformed point of the bullet, which has dug into the thick glass like a worm, catches the sun.

Not so far away, on the roof of another tall building, I notice two white dots. They catch my eye because the white stands out against the dark background in a part of the view that is still shaded and as cold as night and does not include any other distinct white. After concentrating on them for a while, I make out two deckchairs in a place that is clearly not intended for sunbathing. They are arranged neatly parallel to each other.

182

It takes more than three hours for the spring sun to reach the deckchairs.

I push in the Flock 28's safety catch. Slide, recoil spring guide. Barrel with chamber, firing pin, sear. I mumble the names of the parts, as calming as a prayer. For lack of a brass rod, I try to clean the pistol by compressing air in my mouth and blasting it out in a well-directed jet.

I remove the cartridge clip from Harry's pistol.

After approximately four hours the shadow slides back over

the white dots. I don't know how warm it was outside on the roof.

Perhaps it was still too cold.

183

I didn't find the last resident.

I put Harry's Flock in his hip holster, then closed it with the press stud. I laid his cap on his chest and put his hands together on his stomach. I cleaned his shoes with the sleeve of my uniform jacket. I took the torch from his trouser pocket. I closed his eyes and left him behind in the study; I didn't say a word. One instant I saw Harry, the next I saw something else and would never see Harry again. Like a piece of wreckage floating in the sea, I drifted through the building. Time swallowed me and spat me out, then picked me up again. I heard myself laugh, so loudly I thought it was funny. I went in search of a window that opened, convinced I was about to suffocate because the air had been used up. All the furniture I could lift was too light to break the glass. I must have slept. I remember looking at my watch and not understanding what I saw, dredging my memory as if searching for the name of an old acquaintance. In a bedroom, over the head of the bed, beneath a gilded frame, engraved on a minuscule copperplate: "Paul Cézanne. Nature morte. Les pommes." I ran my finger over the apples, tracing their outline, imagining Cézanne's concentration. The banality of art above a bed. The sheets no longer smelt of anything, neither did the pillows. One afternoon my mind was so clear I saw everything at once. The feeling that all objects were converging, glittering, on my retina. I didn't need to focus, one metre away or ten, the sharpness and brightness of the world was overwhelming; I was its focal point. I stuffed a dark-green leaf from a shrivelled pot plant in my mouth, chewed on it briefly then quickly swallowed. I repeated my name in the dark. It appeared before my eyes, dangling there like a carrot on a string.

I didn't find the last resident.

The last resident found me.

184

I feel a hand on my shoulder. It is astonishing how much a hand on a shoulder can say. This one is as self-assured as the guard's bearlike paw, but lacks – despite the complete, breath-taking surprise – all semblance of hostility. It is as if the hand, through its purposeful touch, is conveying its apologies for the intrusion circumstances have compelled it to make. It pushes me down on the spot, not wrenching the joint but forcing me to think for a second without moving, so that I judge the gesture correctly and relax again immediately, at the very start of this imposed reflection, because I am not being overpowered at all – I mustn't think that – on the contrary, I am being invited to turn around calmly, without fear or aggression, to face someone who has emphasized their lack of malice.

Even before I've finished turning my head, I encounter the wave of air the resident has set off by moving in my direction and which now, with a delay, washes over me. The air is tinged with his perfume. a multi-layered scent, which is elegant and discreet, but as strong as an opiate: after a single breath it has reached my toes, intoxicating me, forcing me to surrender. Ginger first, followed closely by citrus, with pepper and, finally, wood adding an unfathomable depth.

I look into greyish-blue eyes without any particular expression. They are framed by heavy, angular glasses. Judging by the modern lines of the interior on the edges of my field of vision, the glasses are deliberately old-fashioned, maybe even genuinely old, vintage. dating all the way back to the fifties or sixties of the previous century. That impression is strengthened by his gleaming bald head and pitch-black, tight-fitting turtleneck pullover.

"I'm Michel."

The words tumble out of my mouth, bouncing like marbles on the concrete floor, and it's only when it's completely quiet again that the resident lays his hand on my shoulder for the second time. What this hand is saying, I don't know. I have no idea. I notice that the resident is slim but nowhere near skinny. His face is sharp, without protruding cheekbones or sunken cheeks. He hasn't been going hungry.

He looks remarkably healthy.

"Are you alright, Michel?"

He lowers his head a little to look deep into my eyes. He's about ten years older than me. Concern, that is what the hand on my shoulder is now conveying, clearly. He is concerned. He is taking pity on me.

"Would you like a glass of water?"

If I let myself go for a moment I would, finally, burst into tears. I would be inconsolable and unable to speak. Nothing would help. He would hug me and not know what to do. I would embarrass him as no-one has embarrassed him before.

"Would you like a glass of water? Are you thirsty?" Without waiting for an answer he turns and disappears around the corner. "Come in," I hear him say.

He is inviting me to enter his apartment. But I am already inside. I am standing in a kind of lobby, which I suspect also contains the lift doors, a bit further along. At the narrower hallway through to his apartment, there is an invisible line; beyond that line are his living quarters. It's a line I won't cross. I know my place. I'm on duty. Without my duties I would never have met the last resident. I pull the knot of my tie tighter and pat my shoulders, arms and chest. I straighten my jacket. Not wanting to be rude, I shuffle up a few steps until I'm at the start of the hallway.

A large bright space extends before me, enclosed on all sides by glass walls: blue sky and white clouds. The full-colour print to the basement's negative. It seems to me as if this space no longer belongs to the apartment building, but is a part of nature. The ceiling is tightly strung sailcloth to protect against the rain and sun, although the bare interior seems designed to easily withstand the elements. The kitchen section in the far corner is gleaming stainless steel and looks more like a laboratory. There, in that same corner, I see green plants swaying on a large terrace. I see a crop and a long row of sticks, and on the ground I see plants coming up.

He is growing his own food!

Unlike Harry and me, he hasn't been living off supplies.

He brings me a glass of water which is undoubtedly purified rainwater. It tastes better than the best wine I have ever drunk. I feel it flowing deep into my belly. Glancing at the embroidered insignia on my chest, he asks, "Are you still here?"

I nod, foolishly. "We came to make sure you were alright."

"I thought everyone left long ago."

I would like to check the time on my watch. I know that later I will want to recall this moment as precisely as possible. I look into the last resident's greyish-blue eyes. I smell his perfume. He talks to me, he exists.

"Harry and I stayed. In the basement."

"You must be the last ones then. As far as I know, everyone else is gone."

The idea that we should take this man downstairs to lock him up in the storeroom and guard him is too insane for words, a delusion of the highest order.

"Harry kept count," I say. "He was certain that thirty-nine residents had left. He knew you were still here. That's why we were looking for you."

"Well, that wasn't necessary," the resident smiles. "I never go anywhere. I've been here the whole time." He gestures at his home. In that instant, as if the two things are related, there is the sound of someone flicking a wine glass with a fingernail, once only. On a long white sideboard, three stylized monitors flick on. Graphs appear: a mountain range, a young mountain range with sharp peaks and deep valleys. Above the mountains, outside behind the glass, a cloud hangs in the sky. This is the highest point of the city. He lives up above everyone and everything, as if in a watchtower.

"Your colleague, Harry, is he coming too? I can offer you some soup. Would you like some soup?" the resident asks with half an eye on the screens. "Pea soup. I made it yesterday so it should be at its best."

I shake my head. "I don't want to delay you."

"The computer can wait. Fifteen minutes here or there won't matter."

Pea soup. The words don't set off any reaction in my mouth. I think I no longer know what pea soup tastes like.

Another ting on the wine glass. A window opens above one of the graphs. On the other screens the mountain ranges make way for scatter plots and three-dimensional histograms. They are moving.

"Excuse me," the resident says, turning on his heel.

I stay standing there uncomfortably at the doorway, taking cover under my cap, in my uniform, feeling a warm gratitude to my uniform, thankful for the pretext of official validity it lends my visit.

"There were days," the resident says, "I forgot I even had a computer. I'm not exaggerating." He peers tensely at the screens, pulls a hand out of his trouser pocket and rubs the curve of his skull as if applying a lotion. "Long ago, Michel. Long ago." Then he pulls a chair on wheels over and sits down.

"I won't disturb you any longer," I say. "I now know that everything's fine. Thank you for the glass of water." I raise the glass, but he doesn't turn around. While I ponder what to do with it, I see him move a hand to the middle monitor, a relaxed, open hand, and tap something with the tip of his slightly bent index finger. Immediately there are beeps, one after the other in quick succession, like falling dominoes, a sweet cheerful digital cascade, which stops abruptly when the screen turns black. A brilliant pinprick of light is imprisoned in the monitor: it flaps long, colourful tentacles to float and sway elegantly through the black, like a ghost delighting in its intangibility.

The resident turns his attention to the right-hand screen.

I put the glass down on the floor.

"Wait," I hear as I'm disappearing into the lobby. His heels click on the concrete and for the third time he lays his hand on

240

my shoulder. This time the hand asks for understanding, but that's not necessary.

"At least take my lift then," the resident says. "It will get you back down in a good forty seconds."

He leads me to the door.

"If anything comes up, let me know. O.K.?"

I step into the cabin and the resident reaches past my chest to the buttons. "You too, sir," I say dutifully in his pointy ear.

My reply amuses him. "I'll do that, Michel."

The last I see of the resident is a gold eye tooth that looks out of place in his mouth and almost turns his broad smile into a sneer.

185

The walls and ceiling are white, padded leather, all sound is absent. There is a very fleeting awareness of motion, the acceleration is probably staged to spare the residents the sensation, however brief, of falling into nothingness. I neither hear nor feel a thing. The panel has two buttons, 0 and -1, and a dark window no larger than a postage stamp. There is no indication of the passing floors. I could just as easily be hanging motionless in the shaft. Nonetheless I am heading for the basement at full speed. After having spent a long time high up in the building, it's as if I'm travelling to the centre of the earth. The basement. The thought of seeing the familiar basement again in just a few seconds! Big warm tears roll into my beard. An enormous sense of relief makes me as light as a feather, floating in the falling cabin. I hear Harry's voice. I feel his moustache against my ear. I feel the strength in the arm he's wrapped around my shoulder. He whispers that I'll be back soon. Do I understand what he's saying? Soon I'll finally be back where I belong. He asks what on earth I'd accomplish by joining the elite. What would I do in a fenced garden where the guards bump into each other and don't even know each other's names? What? He wants me to tell him that. What would that teach me? He says my challenge is here in the basement, in the emptiness, more than a thousand square metres of it. How big had I wanted my challenge to be? Maybe I was born to be a guard. It's a possibility I can't exclude. Yes, this is my last chance, Harry says, but that doesn't mean I haven't ended up in the right place after all. Some people find their place quickly, others at the very end. Mine is here at the entrance to this building and I mustn't forget it. I have 29 cartridges, Winchester, 9mm, and a Flock 28 in excellent condition. It was wrong of us to turn away from the entrance, Harry says, a gross error, but no matter what's happened in the city and the basement in the meantime, my precision and 29 cartridges will get me to the storeroom. Waiting for me there are 2,250 cartridges, corned beef and drinking water. That's all I need. I have to prepare myself for a big adventure; what's gone before will pale by comparison. Every second, a test. The door is about to slide open. Like the acceleration, the deceleration will be gradual. I won't feel it in my bowels. I have to be ready because forty seconds don't last much longer than this. Harry hugs me, squeezing the air out of my lungs. After a kiss on my forehead, he arranges my cap at the prescribed angle. I've been away, he says solemnly. But now I'm back again.

PETER TERRIN was born in 1968 and is the author of two volumes of short stories and four novels. *The Guard*, a winner of the European Literature Prize 2010 and shortlisted for the A.K.O. and Libris prizes, is his first to be translated into English.

DAVID COLMER is the prizewinning translator of novels by Gerbrand Bakker, Arthur Japin and Dimitri Verhulst.